RESCUING ABBEY

KING'S RANCH ~ BOOK 5

DANIELLE HART

FOR THOSE WHO KNOW ME PERSONALLY

I know you are being supportive but you do not have to read this book if you don't want to. If you don't think you can handle a straight face the next time you see me after reading steamy menage scenes, then put the kindle down and walk away.

GET THE FREE PREQUEL

Want to read how King's Ranch all began? Jessie has her own steamy story about meeting and falling for Stefan and Mikel.

The prequel, *Tempting Jessie* is not for sale anywhere, but you can get it when you sign up for my email newsletter!

Click on the link above or pop over to my website at https://www.authordaniellehart.com

ABBEY

*T*hunk, thunk, thunk.

My head against the steering wheel was the only thing that felt real at this moment. I was stranded on the side of the road in the middle of nowhere, Texas, with no gas or cell service. The sun heated the car, and I wondered how long it would be before I cooked alive in the confined space.

I groaned. It was my fault for being distracted.

Walking in on my boyfriend fucking another woman in our bed completely took over my thoughts and, if I'm being honest, my common sense. All I remembered was leaving him a note saying, *we are over*, running out of the apartment, and getting away as fast as I could. As much as I wanted to yell and cry, confronting him would only make things worse.

I needed my best friends. I had to talk to them, had to see them. So, without any planning or a second thought, I put my car into drive and headed toward King's Ranch. I knew Blake and Grace would help me. Even if it was with a side of 'I told you so.' My chest tightened thinking about all the times they had warned me about Jeff.

I glanced at my phone for the umpteenth time. Only ten minutes had passed since I'd looked. Still no freaking service. A pitiful moan escaped my lips, and my head dropped against the steering wheel again.

I'd driven straight from Georgia without stopping for more than gas and food. I hated stopping. It gave me too much time to think.

Without the distraction of driving to consume my waking thoughts, memories of yesterday took over. I'd had the trip planned to visit my mother for months, and I had the best time catching up with her. She peppered me with questions about my future—ones I deflected, like usual. I met her new boyfriend, and when things between them started to spice up, I decided it would be best to let them have their privacy.

I loved my mom but seeing her and her boyfriend's enthusiasm for each other was a little too much. I'd gotten it into my head that surprising Jeff sounded fun. He had mentioned during our talk the night before that he was stressed. Like an idiot, I'd hoped me coming home early would help.

A shiver ran down my spine, and it wasn't from the sweat coating my skin. I needed to stop thinking about him.

I took a small sip from my bottle of water. Survival mode cautioned me to ration everything since I'd been stranded for more than an hour and not a single car had passed by.

What was I going to do?

More than once I thought about walking, but I didn't know how far I'd make it or even how far away my destination was. The spacious green fields to my right were mesmerizing, and the slightly wooded fields to my left were eerie. I couldn't help imagining what might come out of those woods after sunset.

There was no way I wanted to be here to find out. I was more of a city girl than a country girl.

A chime from my phone broke through the silence in the car. My lips pursed together as my gaze caught the reminder to text Jeff. He always made me check in with him at least four times a day if we weren't together, which wasn't very often. He rarely let me out of his sight unless he was at work. I quickly swiped away the reminder, then went in and deleted the thing altogether. I didn't need it anymore.

A tap on the window echoed through the car, and I screeched, jumping a foot out of my seat.

"I am so sorry to startle you, ma'am. Can I be of assistance?" A thick, gruff Texas drawl had me turning to my window.

Holy hot cakes. A tall, broad-shouldered man stood outside my door. I rolled the window down and shielded my eyes to get a better look at the uniformed officer. His fitted, short-sleeved uniform shirt exposed his muscled forearms, his right one covered in tattoos. His jeans were molded to his frame, gripping his thighs and showing off the hard muscles underneath.

He took a step to his right and leaned against the top of the car, casting a shadow across my face.

What a gentleman.

3

"Um… I think I'm lost. I feel like I've been on this road for forever, and there's been nothing for miles. I was on my way to King's Ranch and ran out of gas." My throat tightened at the reminder of why I was stranded. "I didn't fill up at the last gas station I passed, and I have no service, so no way to call anyone, which also means I'm without my GPS," I rambled, unable to stop myself.

His face blurred as tears welled in my eyes.

"It's going to be okay, ma'am." He held out his hands, keeping his voice calm and low.

"Abbey. Please call me Abbey." I took a deep breath and let it out slowly. I really didn't want to freak out in front of Officer Sexypants, but it was looking less likely that wouldn't happen. Now that I knew I wasn't going to die on the side of the road, my body trembled, and my breath quickened. If I couldn't pull myself together, I was going to fall apart. There was no way this day could get any worse.

"Abbey." He waited until my panicked eyes met his. In a soothing tone, he continued, "I'm Officer Bennett. Do you see the fields to your right?" He pointed behind me.

I glanced at the never-ending piece of land. "Yes. I swear it's mocking me." I grumbled to the dark-haired stranger, suddenly feeling calmer as I watched the grass sway back and forth.

"That property is King's Ranch. You're only a few miles from the entrance. Why don't you hop in my car, and I'll take you the rest of the way?"

I whipped my head around to face him. "Oh, no. I don't want to inconvenience you. If it's really only a few miles, I'll walk."

His jaw clenched. "This heat is too brutal for you to be walking that far. And it's not an inconvenience. I was on my way there."

I crossed my arms over my chest, hating that I couldn't immediately trust him. After Jeff's deceit, I wondered if I'd ever trust my instincts again. "I don't mean to sound ungrateful, but how do I know you are who you say you are?"

His perfect lips curved into a big smile, and he tilted his head in an acknowledging nod.

I glanced in my rearview mirror, noticing his police car. In all likelihood, he was exactly who he seemed. And he wouldn't be doing his job if he let someone in need walk away instead of helping them.

He pulled out his badge to prove who he was. "If you'd like, you could listen to me radio in your location. Would that help?"

I nodded. "Thank you so much. I can't believe how stupid I am for letting this all happen." I grabbed my purse and messenger bag from the passenger seat. I rolled the window up and took my car key out of the ignition—not that it was doing anything. I opened my door to find Officer Bennett waiting patiently with his hand extended. His eyes were hidden behind his sunglasses, but the corner of his lips twitched in a friendly smile, and I accepted his help.

He squeezed my hand before holding out his other one. "Let me take your bag for you."

"You're not going to run off with it now, are you?" I half joked. He was still a stranger, and I was in the middle of nowhere.

A chuckle escaped his lips, almost too quiet for anyone to hear. If there had been any other sounds besides the birds chirping in the distance, I would have missed it.

Officer Bennett walked me to the passenger side of his patrol SUV and opened the door. I climbed in, and he nestled my bag on the floorboard by my feet before carefully closing me in and walking around to the driver's side.

He slipped inside the vehicle and fumbled with his radio.

"121 to communications." His deep voice echoed in the small space.

"121, go ahead," a woman responded on the radio.

"It's a 10-8 at this location. I'm 10-42." Officer Bennett finished the call.

"What brings you to King's Ranch?" he asked once he clicked off his radio. There was something about him that had a calming effect.

"I'm visiting some friends. Blake and Grace Henderson. Do you know them? They told me this town was small, but I don't know if everyone really knows everyone like the saying goes."

Officer Bennett smiled. "Yes, I know them." His eyebrows knitted together. "Do they know you're coming?"

"It's a bit of a surprise. They keep asking me to visit them, and I just happened to have some extra time at the end of a previous trip. So I thought, why not?" My forced smile slipped. I was a terrible liar.

"Why don't we call them and let them know I'm bringing you over?" he suggested.

The corners of my lips dropped. "I can't. The stupid thing hasn't worked for hours, or I would have called them to come get me." I shook my phone at him.

"That's okay. I'll call them. Only some carriers provide service all the way out here." Officer Bennett pulled out his cell and dialed a number. The Bluetooth in the SUV picked up the call, and Blake's voice rang through the speakers.

"Hey, Duke. What's up?"

"Hey, Blake. I picked up a woman on the side of the road. She says her name is Abbey and she was on her way to see you."

"Abbey? Are you sure that was her name?" Blake's voice lowered a few octaves.

"Blake. It's me, Abbey," I answered when Officer Bennett—Duke—gave me a questioning look. Duke was a good name for Officer Sexypants.

"Oh my God. Abbey, what are you doing here? You didn't tell me you were coming," Her voice rose in pitch. It was the tone she used when she was worried.

"It's a long story, but I thought I'd surprise you and Grace."

"I wish you would have told us. Grace and I are away at a horse show. We're on our way back, but we won't be there until tomorrow afternoon." Regret coated her words.

"Oh, okay." I couldn't keep the disappointment out of mine. I really needed her and Grace right now. A rustling came through the phone and I glanced over at Duke, my brow creased in confusion. He shrugged his shoulder.

Muffled voices came through, but not well enough to make out.

Without either of my friends home, I should get Duke to drop me off in town and find a cheap hotel to stay in. It would also give me a chance to find someone to get gas to my car, so I could drive it the rest of the way to the ranch.

"Sorry, I had to put you on speaker. You can stay at my house until we get in. Duke can show you where it is. You'll have to sleep on the couch since the guest room is being turned into a nursery, but Gavin will be there, and Travis should be home soon. Duke, if you're not too busy, could you introduce Abbey to everyone?" Blake asked.

"Or you can stay at my house. Scott and Ty are coming back today from their cattle rotation, but you can use the guest room. I'll let them know you're staying," Grace chimed in, and my spirits lifted a little. I couldn't wait to see them, but I wasn't sure how I felt about staying in their homes without them. I knew I could trust Blake and Grace's men, but I hadn't met them yet, and it made me uneasy. Meeting the men felt like it was a big deal, and Blake and Grace needed to be the ones to make the introductions. I knew their men loved them, but I still didn't know the full details of how their relationships worked. Jeff always kept my conversations with the girls short, so we never had the chance to have full-on girl talk.

"It's fine. I'll call an Uber to take me to town and find a hotel." I twisted my hands in my lap.

"Sorry, ma'am, but this *is* a small town. We don't have Uber or cabs or anything like that," Duke said, eyes glued to the road as we headed for King's Ranch.

I let out a sigh, and my shoulders drooped. "You

should turn around, and I'll sleep in my car for the night then." Maybe if I rolled the windows down a little, I could get a breeze to come in, but then I'd have to fight off the bugs.

Grace and Blake's voices jumbled together as they told me how wrong it was for me to even think about doing that.

"Nonsense. She'll stay with me until you guys get back." Duke's firm voice echoed around the cab, silencing everyone. He clenched his jaw and glanced at me.

"Duke, are you sure?" Blake asked.

"I'm sure. I was on my way home from work when I saw her, and I have the next three days off, so she won't be alone. I'll watch out for her until you guys get here tomorrow, and then you can work out whatever arrangements you want." Duke pulled the SUV off to the side of the road and looked at me. "If that's all right with you, of course."

His words bounced around in my head. They were all letting me choose what I felt comfortable with. Tears burned the back of my eyes, but I blinked a few times to push them away. I was finally beginning to see how many of my choices had been taken away from me while I was with Jeff.

"I'll stay with you until they get back. Thank you."

Having Office Bennett in the house with me made me feel a little more at ease with staying in a new place. Duke was a stranger too, but oddly enough, I didn't feel as uncomfortable about being alone in his house for the night. Maybe it was that he was a law enforcer, or maybe it was because we had already been through introductions, but it was different.

"That's settled then. Abbey will stay with me tonight, and you ladies need to drive safe. I don't want to be getting any calls in the middle of the night." Duke pulled onto the road.

"You got it. Thanks, Duke," Blake said.

"Can't wait to see you tomorrow, Abbs," Grace squealed at the end.

"Bye, guys," I called out before Duke pressed the end call button. "Thanks, Officer Bennett. You didn't have to offer your place to me."

"Duke. And it's the least I can do." He glanced at me before jerking his chin to the windshield. "Welcome to King's Ranch, Abbey."

My jaw dropped as Duke pulled into the entrance. We drove under the massive archway over the dirt road and continued on toward a group of buildings. Green pastures lined both sides of the road—these with horses in them, unlike the ones I'd been staring at for hours.

The driveway opened to a number of large buildings. I could tell two of them were barns on my right, and there was a large mansion on the left.

"The big house belongs to the Kingstons," Duke said, pointing out the windshield. "We have the training arenas behind us now. And the structure behind the barns is the dining hall."

I was in complete awe at the sheer size of this place. Now I understood why the girls had decided to stay here, apart from finding the loves of their lives.

"Are those houses?" I pointed into the distance.

"Yes. The staff who have families all have their own houses on the property. The others stay in the bunkhouses."

"I'm not barging in on your family by staying with you, am I? You mentioned your place. I'm assuming it's not the bunkhouse." I whipped my head to face him. My stomach twisted thinking about intruding on his family.

"No. When I'm not working as an officer for the town, I work security at the ranch. Liam and I share the house. He's with Blake and Grace, so you won't have to worry about him."

My shoulders relaxed a fraction.

Duke pulled off from the large dirt area and followed a well-worn path around the side of the barns to a row of widely spaced houses. Parking in front of the first house, he jumped out and made his way around to the passenger side. Before I could finish unbuckling my seatbelt, Duke had the door open and shouldered my messenger bag.

"Why this house?" I asked as he helped me from the car.

"It's easier for me to get in and out of here in a hurry if I need to."

"That makes sense." I followed Duke up the front steps leading to the porch.

He opened the front door and stepped aside so I could enter. "And this is my home," Duke said, closing the door behind us. "I hope you're a dog person," he said, right as a black and white fluffy dog pranced over and started licking my hands. I kneeled and greeted the friendly pooch. "This is Jax. Liam and I got him a few months ago."

I looked at the border collie in front of me, and my

heart melted as he tilted his head to the side, tongue hanging out the side of his mouth. I'd always wanted a dog, but Jeff never let me have one.

Swallowing the lump in my throat, I realized how unreal my life was. I ran from a cheating boyfriend right into the arms of a hot stranger. Today felt more and more like a dream as it went on.

DUKE

*S*tupid, stupid, stupid.

When I saw the car on the side of the road, I never would have imagined I'd end up taking the lone woman home with me.

But why did I invite her to stay in *my* house?

I knew why. Because my mother would hang me by my ears if I wasn't a gentleman. It was ingrained in my DNA. A gentleman looked after a girl who was stranded and alone. Also, she didn't seem too thrilled with the idea of staying at either Blake or Grace's houses without them being there.

I was really hoping to come home and enjoy my night alone. I didn't have to worry about going to work tomorrow. Liam was away for the night, so I had the house to myself.

Except now I had company. I could only pray I wouldn't end up regretting inviting the young woman.

Abbey walked into the front room, Jax hot on her

heels, and turned to face me. "This place is nice." Her surprised tone had me taken aback.

Nice? My place was more than nice. It was masculine and roomy and clean and organized. It was way better than *nice*. Deep, rich woods ran throughout the house. The floors were all hardwood. The chairs and tables were thick mahogany, as well as other matching pieces around the house. We'd worked hard to make the house perfect for when we found the right woman to share it with.

Abbey spun around and walked over to the fireplace. Her hand touched the mantel as she took in the few pictures that lined the top. One of the small group of us who helped start King's Ranch, one of Liam and Grace at the Olympics just a few months ago, an old one of Gavin, Travis, Jessie, and I when we were teenagers, and another of Liam and Blake when they were younger.

I placed Abbey's messenger bag on the sofa before standing beside her. "Shall I give you the tour?"

A shy smile graced her face, and she nodded.

Weaving through the living room and kitchen and the hallway, I showed her where my bedroom was and Liam's. It honestly wasn't that big of a house to begin with. Liam and I had decided that when we expanded the family, we would add on, but years later, we were still in the three-bedroom house we started with and had no prospect of a woman to settle down with.

Stopping in front of the guest bedroom, I opened the door and stepped aside for Abbey. "This is the guest room where you will be staying. The bathroom is across the hall there," I said, indicating the darkened room behind us.

Abbey strolled into the room and looked around. It

was pretty empty. Liam and I never had visitors, so we hadn't put much effort into decorating it besides the basics—a queen bed, a dresser, and a nightstand. There was a bookshelf with our overflow of books, mainly Liam's murder mysteries. As if reading my mind, Abbey took a gander at the shelves.

"Are these all yours?" Her petite frame was more noticeable standing in front of the massive bookshelf. Her long, dark hair flowed down her back and stopped at her waistline. Her jeans cupped the swell of her butt nicely, and I could see streaks on the denim but couldn't tell what they were from.

"Those are Liam's. He loves to read." I rubbed the back of my neck.

"What do you do in your spare time then?" She gazed up at me.

"I usually binge the TV. Mostly turn on the sports channel so I can clear my head." I shrugged. It was a Thursday night, and there was a football game on, but I didn't need to watch it. I glanced at my watch. "Did you grab dinner yet?"

"Umm, no. I hadn't even thought about that." Her cheeks took on a rosy tint.

"I was going to put in a frozen pizza, but we can go to the dining hall and see what the guys have whipped up."

I immediately regretted giving that option when Abbey's forehead scrunched and she shook her head.

"If you don't mind sharing, I'll have the pizza. I'm not picky."

I held my hands up. "We can have the pizza. I'm pretty sure Blake and Grace have told you plenty of stories about the dining hall." I tried to lighten my voice and show her I wasn't going to pressure her with anything. To be honest, I was all for not having to deal with all the yahoos in the dining hall. The men tended to get a bit rowdy after a long day of work on the ranch. The single men especially. I just wanted to relax.

Her deep breath came out in a whoosh. "Thanks. It's been a long day. I don't know if I have the energy to meet a bunch of people." She licked her lips, and my eyes tracked the pink tip as it made its way across her mouth. This was not the time for me to get sidetracked. She had enough to deal with and didn't need to worry about me hitting on her.

Giving her a quick nod, I mumbled, "I'll preheat the oven, and you can make yourself at home."

I could feel the heat of her body following me until we parted ways at the kitchen entrance. Abbey was a friend of the girls, and I needed to make sure she had everything she needed. Blake and Grace trusted me with her, and I would damn sure keep my thoughts and hands in check.

"Is pepperoni okay with you?" I called from the kitchen.

"Pepperoni is my favorite," she answered from the kitchen breakfast bar. I nearly jumped out of my skin. This was not good. I was normally so in tune with my surroundings, but she had consumed my thoughts. I was no longer paying attention to anything else. I had expected her to go to the living room, but she had quietly taken a seat on one of the stools. Heat laced my veins as I watched her eyes track my every movement. No one had ever paid attention to me this closely before. It felt weird, but in a good way.

"Sorry," she said. "I didn't mean to startle you."

"It's fine. I thought I heard you in the other room."

A tiny giggle escaped her lips. Pulling the pizza from the freezer, I made quick work of getting it prepped for the oven as it preheated. "Can I get you anything to drink? Water, Coke, whiskey?"

"A Coke, please. Is there anything I can do to help?"

"You really don't have to."

She raised an eyebrow. "You're letting me stay with you. It's the least I can do."

I fought a grin, liking that she spoke her mind. "You can set the plates out." I handed her two plates, as well as forks and napkins. "You can choose where we eat."

Placing the pizza on the rack, I set the timer and went in search of Abbey. I stopped short in the doorway as I watched her carefully fold a napkin into what looked like a hat. It was so sweet to see the care she used for such a small thing. Pizza wasn't a fancy dinner, but a simple touch like that showed me the little things were important to her. I went back into the kitchen and poured two Cokes into glasses and added some ice to them.

"The remotes are on the side table if you want to pick out something to watch." I brought our drinks out and set them on the coasters Abbey had dug up. Funny how Liam had insisted we have them, but we never used them.

"Is there anything you don't like to watch?" Abbey looked at the three remotes sitting on the side table and then at me. "Umm…"

I grabbed the smallest one and turned the TV on, then

grabbed the next one and turned on the stereo. Handing her the TV remote, I settled on the couch and watched as she scrolled through the channels. When she looked at me, I realized I hadn't answered her question. "I don't like reality TV."

"Not even the cooking shows?"

"Those I can deal with, but not Housewives or those singing competitions."

"What about the prime-time cop shows? You know, being a cop and all, do you like those?" Her eyebrows ticked up.

"I don't like those either. I can't get into them. Being on the job all day, I want to get away from it."

She flipped through the channels some more, stopping on a network channel currently showing a commercial. It was the station scheduled to televise the football game I had hoped to watch tonight. *Score*.

"It's Thursday. Isn't there a game on tonight?" She eyed me over her shoulder.

"There is. If that's what you want to watch."

"I haven't been able to watch a game in so long." A smile lit her face. She placed the remote on the table and tucked her feet onto the couch. *Well, fuck me*, a woman after my own heart. I smiled to myself. This tiny little thing was full of surprises. Jax jumped up and settled on the middle cushion between us.

We dug into the pizza and watched the game. I couldn't stop my gaze from seeking her out. We rooted for the same team, and it was fascinating watching her excitement over the game. She called the refs out on bad plays, cheered when the team did well, and even jumped up and down after a well-earned touchdown. My night of wanting to relax and veg out on the couch watching sports still became a reality. Little did I know how much better this night was going to turn out.

Having the little brunette on the couch beside me was a refreshing change. There was something about her that was oddly comforting. Opening up to new people wasn't easy for me, but with her sitting next to me, I felt like I was at ease. Almost like I'd known Abbey more than just hours, for years. I could feel the edge from the workday slipping away and wanted to sit around, doing nothing, with Abbey.

It scared the crap out of me. I wasn't ready to open my life to someone yet, not even the pretty woman only inches from me.

Abbey stifled a yawn as she uncurled from the cushion. Her arms stretched over her head when she stood, and a moan escaped her lips. "Sorry. I didn't mean to do that."

"It's okay. It's been quite a day," I said, fighting my own yawn. I would have gone to sleep before the game ended, but I was in no rush to leave Abbey's presence. As my eyes grew heavy from exhaustion, I knew I couldn't stay awake much longer.

"Can I get you anything?" I asked when we got to her bedroom door. Jax barged his way into the room and made himself at home on the bed.

Her hand flew to her forehead. "I forgot my bag in the trunk of my car."

"It's okay." The image of her in my clothes flashed through my mind, and my cock grew hard. "I'm sure we have things around the house you can borrow. Let me hunt around."

It took a few minutes of searching, but I found a spare toothbrush, Liam's travel shampoo and conditioner, and an old t-shirt and boxers of mine she could sleep in.

"Is there anything else you think you might need?" I handed her the pile of supplies.

"I don't think so. You've been so great about everything. I'm sorry to be such a burden."

"It's not a big deal. We can go get your bag in the morning," I grunted. "Come on, Jax. Let's leave her be," I called, but Jax stayed firmly on the bed.

"Could he stay with me?" Her eyes pleaded. Within their depths, I noticed flashes of hesitation and maybe a little fear. She was in a strange place, with a stranger, after a stressful day. It was understandable. If she felt more comfortable having Jax with her, then who was I to say no?

"Only if you want him to." Was it ridiculous to be jealous of a dog?

She nodded quickly.

"Then it's absolutely okay." I smiled at her. "Goodnight."

"Goodnight," she whispered back. Looking up at me through her eyelashes, I could see a tiny flare of heat flash in her eyes. Her tiny pink tongue poked out and licked across her bottom lip before she worried the plump flesh with her teeth. I wanted to pull it between my teeth before I dove my tongue in to meet hers, but I couldn't. I needed to walk away.

I strode down the hall, my steps hurrying faster with

each new thought of her. Of what she was wearing or the sound she'd make as I entered her. I held back my groan. I needed to get out of here. The urge to turn around and see her one last time burned my chest. I clenched my hands, my nails digging into my palms to force myself to continue to my bedroom. Once through my door, I shut it behind me and paced back and forth across my carpeted floor.

I only had to get through this night. She would be out of my hair tomorrow after Blake and Grace returned.

STRETCHING my arms over my head, I moaned as all my muscles woke up. Glancing at the clock, it was six in the morning. I blinked away the rest of the fog and realized I'd slept through the night. No nightmares, no horrible flashbacks or episodes. My PTSD usually manifested in some shape or form at night, but it hadn't. The warm image of a beautiful brunette was quickly fading away.

I pulled on my running shorts and tank, then went to the kitchen to leave a note on the counter for Abbey for when she woke up. I slipped on my shoes, opened the front door, and turned, expecting Jax to be there to come on our morning run, but he was still sleeping with Abbey. I shrugged and headed out.

The fresh air cleared my head, while the steady pounding of my feet on the dirt calmed my nerves. This morning was different. I didn't need it like I'd needed it before. My nerves weren't shot from horrible dreams. I wasn't running them over and over in my head. I was disappointed the dream from last night wasn't lingering in my head like the others had.

I made my final lap around and up the front steps. The house was still and dark, so I went into the shower and dressed in fresh clothes. My phone chimed on the dresser. It was Chase, the owner of the auto shop in town, letting me know he was on his way to pick up Abbey's car. She said it ran out of gas, but the car looked old and beat up. I wanted to make sure nothing else was wrong with it before she made any more long-distance travels.

If he was leaving town now, then I had just enough time to grab something for breakfast to bring back for Abbey and me. I didn't want to wake her just yet. She'd had a rough day and probably needed to rest.

In the dining hall, I grabbed pastries and bagels that were out on the counter. Since Jessie was gone, there was no one to make the usual buffet. I would have rather filled up on eggs and bacon, but I'd take the carbs too. Maybe Jax and I could run a few extra laps tomorrow to work them off.

I hurried home, devoured my share of breakfast, and glanced at the clock on the wall. It was time to meet Chase with the tow truck and get Abbey's bags. I didn't know if she wanted to come with me, but I needed to make sure I got everything she needed if she wasn't.

An overwhelming need to care for her rose unexpectedly in my chest. I barely knew her but couldn't stop the feeling that I'd do anything to keep her safe. With my thoughts so unsettled, I shifted from foot to foot outside her door. My hand froze in the air, and my mouth went dry.

Just knock, I repeated to myself. After what felt like hours—but was likely minutes—I rapped my knuckles on the door.

The faint rustling of the bed covers twisted my gut. Immediately, the images of her lying in bed seared into my brain. My hands clenched and unclenched by my side as I fought to shove down the rising tide of desire that surged through me.

When the door opened, my breath stalled in my chest. The shirt I'd loaned the cute little brunette hung on her petite frame. The neck hole stretched wide enough that it draped off one shoulder. I had to press my palm into my thigh to fight the urge to run it through her hair.

Fuck me.

My cock pushed against the zipper of my jeans. I needed to get away before I scared her or made her think I'd invited her to stay for something nefarious.

"Good morning. I'm on my way to meet the tow truck for your car. Do you want to come, or do you want me to get some things for you?" My eyes zeroed in on the unmade bed, and my dick twitched.

"If you could grab my bags from the trunk, that would be great. There should be two." Abbey ran her hands through her hair, trying to tame the mess. It was adorable. *She* was adorable.

I gave a stiff nod. "Sure. I left my number on the kitchen counter, along with breakfast. If you think of anything else you might need from the car over the next thirty minutes, call me. I won't be too long." I caught movement out of the corner of my eye and glanced at the bed. Jax's head popped up from behind a wad of covers. He must have slept with her all night. Lucky dog.

"Thank you. I think I might take a shower, if you don't mind." Abbey's cheeks tinted a rosy color.

"If you need more than the little bottles I brought last night, feel free to use whatever is in there," I grunted, trying not to picture her taking a shower. Naked.

I really needed to get out of here. Maybe once Liam was home, he could talk some sense into me.

In an attempt to keep my mind off my beautiful house guest, my gaze shifted down her body but stopped before it landed on the floor. The bottom of my shirt hit her mid-thigh, and her bare legs continued the rest of the way, shoving my desire for her into high gear until I noticed a yellow and purple bruise on her thigh.

It took everything in me not to react. Logic told me it might have been nothing, but instinct told me it wasn't. I needed to dig deeper. The sweet woman standing before me needed my protection. And I'd do anything to keep her safe.

ABBEY

*T*he warmth in my belly settled between my legs. It wasn't my sleep-clouded mind that imagined Duke's eyes wandering up and down my body.

My shoulder hit the doorframe as I watched him stride down the hall to the front door. His jeans looked like they were made for him, cupping his ass perfectly. His broad shoulders stretched his light gray shirt, molding it to every muscle in his back. I licked my lips and sighed quietly. Duke was one dreamy officer. The vivid dreams he'd starred in last night replayed in my head.

Ahh.

Something cold and wet pressed against my calf. Jax sat beside me, his tongue hanging out of the side of his mouth. I gave his head a few scratches.

"I guess you need to go out, don't you, bud?" I asked, and Jax licked my hand. "Okay. Let's go." Jax bumped against my leg as he rushed by me toward the door. My bare leg.

My entire body heated from head to toe.

Oh. My. God.

I had no pants on.

Duke saw me with no pants on.

I smacked my palm to my forehead and groaned. It hadn't dawned on me what I was wearing when Officer Sexypant's eyes had been wandering. Wiping my hand down my face, I took a deep breath and straightened my shoulders. I couldn't change what happened, so I needed to put it out of my mind.

I threw on my jeans and let the dog lead the way.

By the time I'd walked Jax, taken a shower, and inhaled the breakfast left for me on the counter, Duke had returned with my bags.

My phone buzzed on the counter, making me jump. I'd forgotten we'd put it there to charge last night.

> Grace: We're hitting the road. Should be there around three.

> Abbey: See you guys soon. Drive safe.

"Was that the girls?" Duke asked after he finished chugging a glass of water. It was hard not to stare. The way his throat worked the refreshing liquid, and the way his muscles bunched with every move he made around the kitchen...

"Yes. They should be here after lunch." I swallowed to keep from drooling. "Did you have anything planned for today you need to do? I can make myself scarce if you want."

Duke's eyebrows scrunched together. "I don't have

anything planned. You're welcome to stay here, or you can explore the ranch. If anyone questions you, just let them know who you are. Grace and Blake talk about you enough around here. I don't expect you'll have any issues."

"I hope it's all good things. Those two are like my sisters. Who knows what they say." I clapped my palms to my cheeks to hide the growing heat. I could only imagine the stories the two of them had been sharing.

"All good so far, but you just got here. Stories tend to come out when everyone is together." Duke's eyebrow rose, and a sexy smirk lifted from the edge of his lips.

I stared at the granite countertop. Those gray eyes of his were too penetrating, and there were things I wasn't ready to share just yet.

"Does that mean there are plenty of stories to hear?" he teased.

I chewed my bottom lip when my eyes landed on his slightly upturned lips and ignored his good-natured question. "I think I'm going to roam around the ranch for a bit." I strode to the guest room to grab a few things. When we drove down the dirt entrance on the way in yesterday, I couldn't believe the beauty of this place. My fingers itched to sketch the landscape.

I grabbed my sketchbook, a few pencils, and my phone before heading out. Jax followed me, but I hesitated at the door. I didn't want to take him out if I shouldn't. "Stay, bud."

"Take Jax with you. He needs to stretch his legs. He missed his morning run," Duke said from where he leaned against the column in the living room.

"He won't run away or anything, will he?" I didn't

know the dog well enough, and I didn't want to have to look after him when I wanted to lose myself in my art. And I didn't want Duke angry with me if I lost his dog. I forced back the shiver that threatened to roll through me. Duke wasn't Jeff, and he hadn't given me any indication he would be.

"He'll be fine. He knows his way around the ranch. We usually let him roam around all day and call him when it's time to go inside. Plus, the way he's glued to your side, I don't think he'll wander very far from you." His smile reassured any doubt in my chest.

"Come on, Jax. Let's get a move on." I opened the door and stepped into the morning sun. Texas heat was brutal, and with fall just days away, it was only just beginning to cool down. I needed to find shade if I was going to stay out long enough to satisfy my need to draw.

I followed Jax as he trotted around the ranch. He squeezed his way into a pasture, and I decided he knew best. I unlatched the gate and continued to follow his lead. My heart leapt when we crested a small hill. The view from the top was breathtaking. The field opened and lush green spread all around me. In the distance, a cluster of cottonwood trees broke up the landscape. I could make out more pastures and a few lone oak trees, like the one that stood near the top of the hill.

This place was so serene. Even with my sketchbook in hand, I desperately wanted my paints so I could capture all the colors blending the scene into the perfect landscape. I circled the oak tree, finding which angle I liked best. It took a few minutes to decide on one, then I sat with my legs crossed and reclined against the solid trunk.

Jax zoomed around the pasture a few times, barking and enjoying himself, before he plopped on the ground next to me. After a few scratches behind his ears, he was already dozing. He was the perfect companion while I sketched.

It wasn't long before a few horses strolled into view, and I added them in. One big brown one meandered to where I was sitting to investigate. A snort startled Jax, but he immediately relaxed after a quick look at our guest. With the gorgeous horse so close, I quickly flipped a page and went to work on capturing him on paper. I'd been around Grace and Blake's horses growing up, but it was peaceful being here alone with the curious gelding. No riding, no training, no expectations... just a calm presence.

It was almost like he sensed it too. After munching on some green grass for a few minutes, the bay horse lay next to the tree, only a few feet away. I smiled and continued my drawing. At times, I scooted closer to the horse to get a better look at a feature and eventually ended up leaning against his strong back instead of the tree. I quickly snapped a selfie on my phone with the intention of sending the picture to the girls, but I still had no service. The bit I'd had before was in the house when Duke had given me the Wi-Fi password during the football game so I could connect for some semblance of communication. Glancing at the time, I realized I'd been drawing almost the entire day, and it had felt amazing.

As I put my phone down, a whistle pierced the air. The horse's ears flickered, and Jax lifted his head. It sounded again, but neither animal paid any more attention. I laughed. "Is someone calling us?" I asked Jax as he put his head on my leg. "I guess we'll stay here and wait for him to come to us."

Not five minutes later, a tall, lean man appeared, walking across the field, and bee-lined in our direction. I didn't recognize him, but as he got closer, I could see his blond hair was cut short, but not as short as Duke's. He had on a fitted shirt that hugged his muscles and show-cased his runner's build.

When he got close enough, a smile broke out on his face, stretching from ear to ear. "So you're the one who is holding my animals hostage." His words were laced with a dreamy French accent, making me want to swoon.

He stopped a few feet away, but I still had to crane my neck to look at him as he stood over me. For a second, I marveled at how safe I felt with him nearby. "They heard you whistle but decided it was more relaxing to stay here with me." Where had that come from? I normally didn't talk to random men, much less flirt with them. It was like he exuded a sense of calm, and the filter that was normally in place was gone.

His smile grew. "I see that. May I ask what you are doing out here?"

I could listen to him talk forever. I let my pointer finger rest on my sketchbook. "Taking in the scenery. What are you doing out here?" I still didn't know who this guy was, but there was something about him that tugged at my memory.

"I came to look for my new houseguest." He winked, his smile firmly in place.

Heat flooded my cheeks. This must be Duke's roommate. He'd mentioned his roommate was away at the horse show with the girls. And if he was here, I had to assume this meant they were back.

Which would mean I wasn't his houseguest anymore. With my friends back, I'd stay at one of their houses. An ache settled in my chest.

I'd have to leave the comfort of Duke's house and separate from this sweet pooch keeping me company. Jax had barely left my side since I got here, and his gentle presence was soothing. I kissed the dog's head and scratched behind his ears before I stood.

"*Pardonne-moi.* Where are my manners? I'm Liam Kilpatrick." Liam held out his hand, and I took it. Instead of shaking it like I expected, he lifted the back of my hand to his mouth and placed a light kiss on my knuckles. *Holy hotness.* Did he just do that? No one had ever kissed my hand like a real gentleman.

"I'm Abbey Kilpatrick." My voice was far too breathy for my liking. Liam smirked, and I realized what I'd just said. "I mean Abbey Bennet." Oh shit, that wasn't right either. I wanted to groan the moment I realized I'd used Duke's last name.

Liam's smirk turned into a full-on grin.

"Ugh. Kill me now." I tried to pull my hand away, but his grip tightened.

"I'd rather not." His voice rumbled through me, making me shiver.

Taking a deep, calming breath, I tried again. "I'm Abbey Young."

"Nice to meet you, Ms. Young." His eyes held mine as we spoke, creating a sense of intimacy.

My body tingled all over. His voice, his gentle touch, his penetrating golden-honey eyes... They wreaked havoc on my body.

"Abbey, please." I pulled my hand from his. Without the contact, I was able to breathe again. Just barely. His stare pinned me in place.

"Abbey." He paused as though gathering his thoughts. Or maybe he was just as affected by my presence as I was by his.

I liked the way my name sounded when he said it. That accent of his probably made every woman turn into a puddle at his feet. I was certainly on my way.

"Are you allergic to anything?" he asked.

"What?" I tilted my head slightly, thrown off by the unexpected question.

"Dinner. Tonight. Seven o'clock. Are you allergic to anything?"

"Umm, pecans. But I thought I'd be staying with Grace or Blake tonight." I tilted my head to the side.

"Not tonight. The girls just got back from a trip away from their husbands. I figured you wouldn't want to listen to them fucking all night long."

A flash of heat raced through my body at his provocative words. "Umm... good point."

"That settles it then." His devastating grin made me want to run my fingers across his lips. "I'll see you at the house. I'm making dinner tonight."

"Are you going to tell me what you're making?" I asked, forcing myself to try to act normal.

"Nope. Come and prepare to be amazed." Liam winked and left without another word.

My stomach did flips as I watched Liam swagger down the hill.

So that was Liam. *The* Liam who Blake had competed with years ago. The guy who was like a big brother to Grace. And the guy who had my insides all tangled up just from looking at him. Now I knew why he seemed so familiar.

Oh God… I was staying with him.

It was hard enough sleeping with Duke in the other room. I was up most of the night, tossing and turning, vivid images of him in my bed. Now Liam was ruining my panties with his dirty-blond locks and sexy smirk.

How though? How could I be attracted to two guys?

How could I even be attracted to one after everything I'd been through?

I took a few minutes to examine my feelings. I figured I'd need more time before I'd be so attracted to someone again. Though I didn't think I'd ever felt like this with Jeff. Maybe when we were in high school. He was my first real boyfriend, and I thought I loved him, but he hadn't piqued my desire in a long time.

Now I was almost dreading dinner. Not only was Liam cooking, which was so sweet, but Duke was going to be there. Sitting at the same table with those two men was going to be the hardest thing I'd ever done. It was going to take everything in me not to combust at the sight of them.

Jax licked my hand, startling me. I scratched between his ears and sat on the grass.

An hour later, I looked up to see another figure waddling through the grass in my direction. "Blake," I shouted, earning a nicker from my companion and a bark from Jax. Grabbing my things, I ran to meet her halfway. "Oh. My. Gosh. Look at you." I wrapped my arms around her pregnant belly as best as I could.

"Abbs, I can't believe you made it out here. What happened? Why are you here? Why didn't you tell us you were coming?" She looked me over from head to toe, then handed me a bottle of water and a snack bar. Blake was my big sister in every way but blood, and I loved how she looked out for me.

"That's a conversation for another day and deserves a bottle of wine and ice cream." Today had been great so far. I didn't want to mar it with talk about Jeff and what he'd done. "Thanks for this." I held up the water and snack.

She gave me another concerned look but didn't pressure me to explain. "Oh… well then, let's get together tomorrow. That way Grace can be there too." Blake looked at her belly, then back to me. "Do you mind staying with Duke another night? I just ran into Liam, and he mentioned having you stay with them tonight since, you know, we've been away from our guys for a week." Her lips turned down, and I could see that she was torn between being there for her husbands and being a good friend.

"Blake, it's fine. I'll stay with the guys another night. Don't worry. It gives me an excuse to get to know Liam." I waggled my eyebrows, hoping to get a laugh from her. I didn't need her to worry about me when she needed to be calm and stress free for the baby.

"Oh my gosh. That's right. You're going to love him,

Abbs. He's such a good guy. I know he will take good care of you." She smiled and squeezed my shoulders.

"He mentioned he was cooking dinner. Should I be worried?" I tilted my head and squinted.

"Don't worry. You are in good hands. I promise. He never let me cook when I was traveling with him."

"That's because you can't cook." I bumped her shoulder with mine as we made our way out of the paddock. "Please tell me he isn't going to make me eat snails or something weird." I stuck my tongue out.

Blake held her stomach as she laughed. "I think you're safe."

LIAM

"*Y*ou failed to mention how gorgeous she was before I went out there." The front door bounced off the wall as I entered the house. I came straight home from meeting Abbey in the paddock.

"I hadn't noticed," Duke mumbled from where he sat on the couch, his head buried in a book. He always made fun of me for reading, but he loved a good adventure book as much as I loved my mysteries.

I'd seen pictures of Abbey from Blake and Grace. Even years ago, I had to admit she was a pretty little thing, but her looks back then were nothing compared to the beautiful woman sitting under that tree with my horse and dog. After hearing about her over the years, it felt like I'd known her forever when I actually knew nothing about her. I'd honestly just imagined her to be another version of Grace since they were the same age.

"Did you go shopping today?" Opening the fridge, I found my answer before he spoke.

"No. I was kind of busy today. I met Chase to pick up Abbey's car." He shrugged. If he didn't get anything in town, then I was short on supplies to make dinner.

"I wanted to make dinner." Sighing, I went to the pantry and looked inside. There were a few things I might be able to whip together to make a decent meal, but would that be good enough for our guest? Why did I care so much?

"You are? What are you making?" Duke looked up from his book.

"I don't know. Someone didn't go to the store, so we have little to work with." I arched my eyebrow.

Setting his book on the coffee table, Duke wandered into the kitchen. He always liked it when I did the cooking, but he did help out, for which I was grateful. Duke opened the fridge again, then proceeded to shut it only a few seconds later. "We could go to the dining hall and see what Jessie might let us have."

It wasn't a bad idea, but it wasn't our best idea either. Jessie, our resident cook and wife to Stefan and Mikel, two of the original founders of King's Ranch, had been in New York with the team helping at the event, so she wouldn't have been able to stock the dining hall, but it was worth a shot.

"Let's go and check it out." I shoved Duke and walked out of the kitchen with him right behind me.

I had to hope that Abbey would stay out long enough for us to get back and start dinner. It hadn't sounded like she'd talked to Grace or Blake yet, but it wouldn't surprise me. They had a lot of unpacking to do.

"Guys, mind giving us a hand with this?" Blake stepped out of the barn as we passed by and shouted.

"How can we help? We were on our way to see what we can mooch off the dining hall," I called as we detoured, stopping in front of Blake.

"Why would you need to do that? Just eat there." Blake crossed her arms the best she could with her eight-month belly sticking out.

"Because I'm making dinner for the three of us, and Duke didn't go to the store today."

"Really?" She arched her eyebrow.

"I had to get Abbey's car towed," Duke grumbled.

I had to wonder if it wasn't because he didn't want to leave without Abbey being back.

"Thank you for helping her. We'll come by and bring her to stay at Grace's as soon as we finish." Blake let her arms fall, and she placed a hand on Duke's bicep, completely oblivious to Duke's stiffening shoulders.

"You don't need to do that," I all but squeaked out. Clearing my throat, I tried again. "We'll keep Abbey another night and let you and Grace settle in with your men." When Blake didn't look convinced, I added with a toothy smile, "Please."

"Why? What's going on? Is everything all right? I should at least go check in on her." She pivoted and started toward our house.

I reached for her arm to stop her, but she slipped from my grasp. "Everything's fine, I promise. Let Abbey unwind before you girls start at it."

Blake stopped and turned to me. "Liam. Something is

up and I want to know. Why do you want Abbey to stay with you?"

"Something's up, all right," Duke teased under his breath, and I shoved an elbow into his ribs. Blake's forehead scrunched.

"Not helping," I muttered out of the corner of my mouth. "I've heard all about her from you and Grace. Duke had the privilege of getting to spend time with her already, and I haven't. You always said she was like a little sister to you. It's my turn to get to know her." I wasn't going to mention how intimately I wanted to get to know her unless I wanted my balls removed. Blake had gone into protective mother mode over the last few weeks, and I wasn't sure I wanted to test her.

"You're not fooling me, Liam. But I do appreciate the space for a night. With these hormones, it's harder than ever to not jump my men every time I see them." Blake turned to Duke. "Are you sure you're okay with one more night?"

Duke grunted with a firm nod.

"Okay then. I'll call Abbey in a few and check in with her. Make sure she's okay with all this too."

"I wouldn't have expected anything less, ma moitie." I held up my finger. "But she's in the paddock with Zeus and Jax."

"She has no cell service out here," Duke added.

"We'll need to fix that." Blake headed toward the paddocks. "Her favorite food is tacos," Blake shouted.

I spun around, meeting Blake's smirk.

Fuck.

She saw right through me.

* * *

SOMEHOW, Duke and I procured enough ingredients to make decent tacos. Not my best work, but if Blake said they were her favorite, then I wanted that to be what she had. When I cooked for her again, I would be sure to wow her with my skills.

Duke chopped the tomato and lettuce, while I sautéed the ground meat.

"Dude, stop checking your phone. It's been two minutes since the last time you checked."

Duke's gravelly voice had me glancing in his direction. He could try to hide it all he wanted, but the more he got worked up, the more of a grouch he was. He was waiting on pins and needles for Abbey to come home just as much as I was.

He was right though. I glanced at the clock on the oven and only another minute had passed. The sun still had an hour before it fully set and the darkness crept in, but my insides felt itchy knowing she was out there alone. Nothing could get to her while on the ranch, but she didn't know the place, and what if she got lost on her way to the house?

The distant sound of barking straightened my spine, and I wiped my hands on a dish towel before making my way to the front door.

Jax came bounding in as soon as the door opened. Before Abbey made it inside, Jax zoomed back outside and circled her, barking happily. His yaps and her laugher made my chest tighten. It was important that whoever stayed with us—a temporary guest or the woman who completed our family—had to get along with and love Jax.

Duke and I had only taken Jax in a few months prior, but he was just as much a part of the family as either of us were. He'd done a lot for Duke, pulling him from his PTSD episodes, and he gave me another companion I could look after.

"Did you have a good day?" I locked the door behind Abbey and Jax.

"It was great. This place is so beautiful. I could spend all day, every day, out there." Abbey beamed as she set her bag on the sofa. "Except it's so hot outside. Is it always this bad?" Her southern drawl was adorable. It reminded me of Blake and Grace's, but it was so much cuter on Abbey.

"It can get worse. Even though it's fall, the heat will get to you. In about a month, we should get some cooler weather." Duke popped his head around the kitchen corner.

"Well, that'll be refreshing. I should have delayed my trip a little longer." She cast her smile in his direction. The corner of his mouth tilted at her sarcasm.

I chuckled and pointed to the couch. "Sit. Relax. Dinner should be ready soon."

"Is there anything I can help with?" Abbey clasped her hands in front of her.

"I think we are good. Duke here is a great sous chef." I nudged Duke as I re-entered the kitchen.

"Fuck you," Duke mumbled under his breath, only making me laugh more. He was easy to pick on because he was a grump, but I knew he understood it was all in good fun. It was how we'd gotten along so well over the years. When I joined the Kingston Equestrian team, I didn't know anyone. But then I met Duke when he came back from the police academy, and we hit it off right away.

"Do you like wine with your dinner, or do would you like something stronger?" I called from my place behind the kitchen island.

"Water is just fine." Abbey strode into the kitchen. She made her way to the cabinet and grabbed a glass. "What are you both having?"

"I'll have water as well," I said at the same time as Duke gave his own answer, "Water, please."

Abbey went to work filling three glasses. "So, what's for dinner? It smells amazing in here."

"Tacos." Duke lined the island with bowls of toppings, and I set the pan of meat on a trivet near the tortillas. "In fact, it's ready when you are."

"Ooh. I love tacos." Abbey rubbed her hands together and danced to the island where the plates were stacked.

"Ladies first." I looked at Duke and winked. She was cute. All excited over a simple meal. I had to remember to file that away. *It's the simple things that count with her.*

Within minutes, we were sitting at the dining room table, stuffing our faces.

"So, Liam… You were at the show with Blake and Grace? Did you win anything?" Abbey asked between mouthfuls.

"Yes, I was there, but I didn't compete."

She tilted her head to the side. "Why weren't you competing?"

"My horse, Zeus, is still getting over an infection. He was the one you were hanging out with in the paddock."

Abbey froze. "Oh my gosh, please tell me I wasn't hurting him. He was laying there, and I didn't think anything of leaning against him." Her eyes grew wide.

"He's fine. Horses lay down all the time to relax." I kept my voice calm, even though I wanted to laugh. She was sweet.

"Then why did you go to New York if you weren't planning on competing?"

I loved that she wanted to know more about me and my work. "I tagged along to support the rest of the team. Plus, with Blake being pregnant, she needed an extra hand out there." Shrugging, I took another bite of my taco.

"I'm not sure how it all works, but aren't you concerned about your standing and points and all that? How many shows have you been out with Zeus being injured?" Her focus was no longer on dinner. My stomach did a flip at having her attention solely on me. I wasn't used to it.

"I'm not worried. We won medals at the Olympics over the summer. We have another year before we need to worry about my standings."

"I can't believe you went to Brazil with Grace. That's so cool." Abbey sighed and rested her chin in her hand. Her eyes were bright as she stared at me.

Duke grumbled, and I chuckled. Was Duke jealous?

"Competing has given me so many opportunities to travel, but it's been nice to have a place like King's Ranch to come home to. Honestly, I wish there were more times

I could just stay and relax without having a packed schedule." These thoughts had been weighing on me more and more lately. I didn't want to think of the word *retire*, but after twenty-plus years of this life, I was ready to slow down. Thirty-five was still a prime age for competing, but I wanted to look forward to other things besides the next Olympics.

"I'm sorry, Liam." Abbey reached across the cherry-wood table and squeezed my hand. The warmth of her touch sent tingles of awareness up my arm.

"That's what the team life is all about, right?" I took a deep breath and tried not to stare at her warm touch. It took everything in me not to place my other hand over hers.

"I have a question." She pulled away and turned her golden-brown eyes toward Duke. "Liam just got home from a trip, so it's understandable, but I would have expected you to have Friday night plans." She pointed to him. "Or did you cancel something because I'm here?"

I was surprised at her directness.

"I'm on a four-day break at work right now. And my plans usually include working around the ranch and relaxing."

"Plus, Duke doesn't socialize very well," I added, earning a glare from him. I shrugged. It was true. He hated going out in public, and his attitude was getting worse every day.

"I don't get out much either." Her voice dropped to a tone so quiet I had to strain to hear her. "Normally, I'm at home with a book or a movie. I try to put my sketchpad away after a certain time, so I don't get too lost."

"Is that what you were doing in the paddock? Sketching?" I'd seen the notebook in her hand, but I'd thought it was a reading one.

"I sketch in my free time." Abbey looked at her plate.

"That's amazing. I have no artsy bone in my body." Duke's deep timbre was smooth instead of its usual gravelly edge. "Were you an art major?"

Abbey nodded. "Nothing came out of it though. No one likes my work. I just do it for myself." Her cheeks took on a fiery tint that reached her ears. I hated that she was embarrassed by what she saw as a lack of success.

"I'd like to see it someday, if you'd show me." This time I reached across to her hand, wanting to comfort her.

Duke nudged her arm. "Me too."

When she looked up, her eyes were glistening. I didn't believe she wasn't any good. Maybe she needed someone who supported her unconditionally to take the next step. I was curious to see what she'd drawn today. Perhaps see how she'd drawn Zeus.

Duke cleared his throat. "What's the plan for tonight?"

"What kind of movies do you like?" I asked. Abbey had mentioned she usually watched movies at the end of the day. We did too. I liked that we all used a movie to unwind.

"I usually go for comedies. What about you?" Abbey finished her taco. "Wait, let me guess. You like horror and suspense?" She shivered as she pointed at me.

I chuckled. "How did you guess?"

She gave me a satisfied look, as though she'd gotten one over on me before dissolving into laughter. "The books in the guest room. Duke said they were yours." She turned to Duke. "And I think you like to watch sport movies?"

"Nope. I like nature documentaries and survival shows." He cocked his eyebrow at her and smirked. It was amazing to see how quickly Abbey had been able to break through his grumpiness.

"But I thought you said you didn't like reality TV?" She titled her head, challenging whatever conversation they'd had previously.

"I don't, but those survival shows are ones I don't consider reality."

"How are those not considered reality shows?" Abbey's laughter filled the dining room and my heart as she and Duke debated TV shows. It was hard to picture the girl I had once thought Abbey to be. Now all I could see in front of me was this beautiful, artsy woman who loved my animals and could put up with Duke's moods.

We were either extremely lucky or in serious trouble.

ABBEY

I blinked and stretched as the sun streamed through the window in the guest room, enjoying the sounds of the morning. It was distant—the lowered voices and footsteps in the outside hall let me know the guys were awake already. My thoughts drifted to them when the knocking started at my door.

Wiggling from under the covers, I padded to the door with the friendly border collie at my feet. Liam stood on the other side, frozen—exactly like Duke had been the day before. My face heated as I glanced down. *Shit.*

I'd opened the door again in nothing but a shirt and underwear. This time it was my clothes and not Duke's. My tank clung to my body, and I realized too late it did nothing to hide my boy shorts from view.

Liam's eyes wandered to mine, and my ears felt like they were on fire. He opened and closed his mouth, reminding me of a fish out of water. I couldn't help but smirk.

Liam cleared his throat. "Umm…"

"Good morning, Liam." Jax squeezed his way between us and sat on my feet, staring up at his owner.

"Tu me tues, dulcinée." Liam ran his hand down his face.

I about swooned on the spot. He was speaking French, and it didn't matter that I had no idea what he said. Heat pooled at my core, and my heart pounded in my chest. "Whatever you say." I leaned against the doorframe. It was probably silly, but he could say anything in French, and my answer would be yes.

Commotion in the other room had me peering into the hallway beyond Liam.

"Where is she? Let me at her." Grace's voice echoed down the hall, seeming to bring Liam to his senses.

"Blake and Grace are here for you," he said, right before Grace barreled past him, nearly tackling me to the floor. Jax yelped and rushed out of the room, followed by Liam after he mumbled goodbye.

"Hi." I laughed through Grace's all-consuming hug. "My ribs," I wheezed when she didn't let up.

"Grace, let the woman breathe." Blake waddled into the room. "And maybe let her get dressed."

When I pried myself from Grace's grasp, I rushed to my bag and pulled out clothes for the day. Blake shut the door, and I quickly changed.

"So, I know you said wine and ice cream, but what about mimosas and cinnamon rolls?" Blake didn't have the patience to wait for me to get dressed. When we were younger, she never wanted to wait. She did what she could to get the gossip out of me as soon as she knew something was wrong. Her thinking was that it was worse to let something fester.

She wasn't wrong. I had wanted to call the girls when I was on the road… and the first time Jeff had hit me. But I let him sweet talk me into thinking it was my fault. And when I realized I needed to get out, I didn't call them. Jeff has beaten me both physically and mentally; I didn't think I was worthy of them dropping everything at the ranch to hurry and be by my side. I knew they would, but I'd convinced myself their life on the ranch needed their attention more than I did.

I nodded before shoving my shirt over my head. "Okay." My stomach growled, and we all laughed. My constant hunger wasn't anything new to them.

"Be back later, boys. We're stealing her for the day," Blake called as we walked out of the house.

Liam and Duke appeared in the living room just before I closed the door. I took one long look at them. Liam winked with a smile, and Duke's jaw tightened.

I sighed as the door clicked shut. Those two were going to drive me crazy. It's like that saying, *you always want what you can't have*. Or in my case, what I *shouldn't* have. I didn't need another guy in my life, let alone two. I needed to find time to learn to be me again.

We fell into light conversation as they led me to a building in the distance. I saw a few cowboys sitting at bench tables, drinking their coffee. The large island that separated what looked like the kitchen from the eating area was lined with food. My eyes widened at the delicious breakfast buffet, and my stomach whined that I hadn't already dug in.

"Jessie, do you have the goods?" Grace asked a tall,

blonde woman standing on the kitchen side of the island. She wiped her hands on her apron and nodded.

"As requested." Jessie reached under the counter and produced a bottle of champagne, then disappeared and returned with a pitcher of orange juice and a plate piled high with gooey cinnamon rolls.

My mouth watered.

Blake led us to a table close by and settled in. I was happy to see Jessie joining us.

"Please tell me you're Abbey." Jessie poured the champagne into mason jars for everyone except Blake, and Grace topped them off with orange juice.

"I am." I took a sip of my mimosa and smacked my lips. Refreshing and delicious.

Jessie let out a squeak. "I'm so glad you're here." Another bone-crushing hug for the morning. "I feel like I already know you with as much as the girls talk about you. They've been so excited for you to visit."

I scooped a sticky-sweet roll from the tray and tried my best to ignore the ache in my chest. They'd mentioned me coming here almost every time we talked, and I turned them down. Controlling boyfriend and all.

I had to let it go. I was here now. Better late than never.

"Enough stalling. Tell us what happened." Blake let me have one bite of my breakfast before diving right in.

"I can leave if you want me to." Jessie started to rise, but I held my hand up and she sat down.

"You can stay." Maybe she could even give an impartial opinion, since I knew how Grace and Blake were going to react to the news.

"I've wanted to call you guys for a while now, but I've just been too scared. Jeff had been getting worse and worse, and I just didn't know what to do." My shoulders dropped, and I stared at my plate. Suddenly, I wasn't hungry. "You know how he was before—always wanting me to check in with him, making sure I did everything he asked me to, never letting me go out with classmates after class. Even though *he* could have a boy's night and *he* could work late."

Blake took a bite of her breakfast, her gaze never leaving mine.

Jessie's mouth dropped into a sad frown. "That sounds awful, girl. No wonder it took you so long to get here. Please tell me you dumped that man."

A chuckle escaped me. It wasn't a laughing matter, but Jessie didn't know the whole story.

"Shhh. Let her finish." Grace smacked Jessie on the arm, then nodded for me to continue.

"Well, it was getting out of hand. To the point that even when I was in class, I had to check in with him when it was over. Then he got upset every time I wanted to visit my classmate. I had put off seeing her, making excuses for why I couldn't for so long. Finally, I couldn't take it anymore and went to see her. She was having a hard time, and I wanted to be there for her. When I came back…" I tried to swallow the lump in my throat. I didn't want the girls to know this, but I had to tell someone. Getting it out there in the open was the only way I could get over it.

"When I got back, he went ballistic and threw things around the apartment. He broke a chair and smashed the remote. That was the first time he hit me." I exhaled.

I said it.

All three gasped and talked over each other. Arms were wrapped around me, and I fought the tears. Their words were blurred together, and I caught only bits: I could handle this. I could get over this. I'd cried enough over that stupid guy.

Taking a deep breath, I struggled to keep my voice even. "At first, I blamed myself, thinking if I hadn't gone to see my friend, then everything would be all right. But eventually, more and more things set him off. After I graduated, he wouldn't let me get a job. He said he wanted me to stay at home where he knew where I was. I'd always thought Jeff was just protective of me, always wanting me near, but now I see it as possessive." My vision blurred, and I looked up at the ceiling. I didn't want to cry again. I'd cried too much already.

"Abbey, why didn't you tell us sooner? You know we would have come and got you." Grace wrapped her arm around my shoulders.

After a few minutes, I realized the whole dining hall had gone silent. Looking around the room, I saw everyone had cleared out but us. I could only hope the men had left before I'd started to cry. That was all I needed—them thinking I was small and weak.

"What was it that made you drop everything and drive here on your own?" Blake leaned as far forward as her belly would allow and grasped my hand.

I reached for my mimosa and took a large gulp. I'd already told them the worst of it. This was the easy part. "I went to visit my mom but decided to come home early to surprise Jeff."

"Oh no. I don't like where this is going," Grace groaned.

"Jeff was fucking another woman in our bed."

The girls gasped collectively.

"I hightailed it out of there. I hopped in the car and headed in this direction."

Blake's forehead wrinkled. "You didn't confront him? Have you spoken to him at all?"

"I left him a note saying we were over. He tried calling me on the first day when I didn't check in, but since then, I've had really spotty service." I shrugged. Ignoring him was not my best plan, but it was also hard to get in touch when my phone didn't work. "Duke gave me the Wi-Fi password, so I was able to see he'd texted me, but I've been ignoring him."

"You know he isn't just going to go away. You need to make sure he knows it's over." Grace crossed her arms. "Jeff was never one to give up easily. I wouldn't be surprised if he tries everything he can to get you back."

"Well, I'm not going back to him. And I'm staying as far away from men as possible."

"You picked the wrong place to do that, girl." Jessie laughed. "This place is teaming with men."

Blake and Grace both nodded.

"Please don't tell anyone about this. I don't want anyone knowing." I worried my bottom lip between my teeth. I didn't need everyone to know I let him abuse me and it took him cheating on me to leave.

"Abbey, I think it might be beneficial if you had a talk with Alex. Her ex-husband is a real piece of work, and she might be able to give you advice." Jessie topped off our glasses. "I know you don't want to tell anyone else, but there are other people on the ranch who can help you with this. And not just the girls."

I tilted my head to the side. "What do you mean?"

"Besides Alex, you could talk to Duke. He's a sheriff. He could probably help in some way, especially if you need to file a restraining order. We could see if the Kingstons can lend a hand. They don't take things like this lightly, even if you aren't an employee." Jessie picked up a roll and waved it around as she talked.

"Don't forget that this place has a lot of muscle. Each and every one of them are very protective of women." The corner of Blake's mouth tilted up. I knew this was weighing heavily on her. We grew up together. Without a doubt, she was blaming herself for all of this when she had nothing to do with it. She tried to warn me in high school about Jeff. It unfortunately took me a lot longer to see what they saw.

I reached for my gooey pastry and took a huge bite. "It was a blessing he did this. Honestly, I haven't been happy for a long time."

"At least you see that." Grace took a bite of her own roll. "Now you can move on and find someone who is worthy of you."

I huffed. That wasn't going to be happening anytime soon. If I couldn't make Jeff happy, who said I was going to be able to make someone else happy? Jeff made a lot of mistakes in our relationship, but in the beginning, it wasn't all bad. Was it me or something I did to change how he treated me in our relationship? No matter how much I tried to say I was, I didn't believe I was worthy of having a dream relationship like these women had.

AFTER CHECKING out Grace and Blake's places, we determined it would be best if I stayed in the women's bunkhouse. I'd be uncomfortable sleeping on Blake's couch, and Grace's guest bedroom was right next to hers. I didn't want to hear her and her men every night and needed to vacate Liam and Duke's place and give them back their guest room.

I packed my bag with the few things I'd unloaded and went to thank my hosts.

"You're leaving?" Liam looked at my bag. "Where are you planning on staying?"

"The Kingstons are letting me stay in the bunkhouse. We didn't think it would be comfortable at either Blake or Grace's place." I set my bag down and joined Liam at the kitchen counter.

"You can stay here. We have the guest bedroom, and you've already stayed here two nights. Why change locations?" He set the cups he was drying down on the counter a little harder than necessary.

I flinched. *Was he getting upset about this?*

Duke smacked Liam on the arm. "She can go wherever she wants to."

Liam gave me a sheepish look.

Jax came over and sniffed my bag. His doe eyes looked up at me, and my heart clenched. I didn't want to leave the dog. I loved having him with me the past two nights.

And if I was being honest, I didn't want to leave the guys either.

"I'm sorry, boy. I won't be far though." I scratched behind his ears. "Thank you for letting me stay, but I don't want to overstay my welcome." I caught Duke's gaze. His jaw twitched, and I noticed his scruff had gotten darker. He must not shave when he is off from work. If it was even possible, he looked sexier.

"You aren't overstaying. You're leaving too early." He looked directly into my eyes.

Unable to pull my gaze away, I sucked in a breath. Duke wanted me to stay?

"You say that now, but if I stay any longer, I'm going to end up claiming Jax." I tried for a joke, but I wasn't sure I had it in me. It had been another emotional day, and my humor meter was at an all-time low.

"Why don't you stay another night at the very least? Tomorrow, we can get your car, and you can decide if you want to stay in the bunkhouse," Duke offered.

It wasn't a bad idea to stay another night. It would beat being alone. The girls mentioned I'd have lots of privacy since no one was currently using the women's side, but when I thought about leaving Duke and Liam, my chest tightened. I'd grown comfortable in the last few days, and I didn't want to leave it just yet.

"Okay. One more night."

Later, I awoke to a noise I couldn't place. Jax jumped from the bed and went to the door. "What is it, boy?" I asked. He looked at me and lay on the floor. A few moments later, the sound happened again. Extracting myself from the covers, I opened the bedroom door and listened.

The sound came again from down the hall. Tiptoeing, I followed Jax and made my way to where the boys' rooms were. I stood quietly, waiting to hear which room it was coming from. When I heard the pained grunting and moaning, my chest started to ache with worry. Jax sat in front of Duke's door and let out a soft whimper.

I rapped my knuckles lightly on the door. "Duke? Are you okay?"

Only a frantic moan answered.

Was he okay? I couldn't tell and didn't know if I should get Liam.

Turning the knob as silently as I could, I opened the door to Duke's room. I'd briefly peeked in when he gave me the tour, so I knew the basic layout. The bed was in the middle of the room, and I could see a dark figure thrashing around.

"Duke?" I whispered.

His movements lessened only a little. I padded to him, letting my eyes adjust to the little light streaming through his curtains.

"Stop. Don't go. Abort mission." His words jumbled together as he mumbled in his sleep.

"Duke. It's okay," I breathed. "It's me, Abbey."

Duke's thrashing settled. "It's too dangerous. Go back." More muttering.

"Duke, you're having a dream." I lay my hand on his forearm, and he quieted. He wasn't awake, but I'd take it over the nightmare he was having. Whatever was happening in his dream was bad. I perched on the edge of his mattress and kept my hand on him.

The clicking of Jax's nails on the hardwood floors drew my attention. Jax was sitting at the door, looking at us. "Good boy. It's okay. Duke was just having a bad dream," I whispered to the pooch, who lay in the doorway. I smiled. He was so intuitive.

I turned to Duke. He was shirtless, and the sheet was bunched around his abdomen. I could see a few silvery scars that peppered his chest and abs. Every muscle that was exposed glistened with sweat. His beard looked even darker in the low light, having not shaved in a couple of days. A few strands of hair clung to his forehead. I gently brushed them away only to have my heart stop when Duke sat straight up.

We gasped collectively. Duke's hand was wrapped around my wrist, his face stopped inches from mine. My body froze for a moment, then relaxed. Duke wasn't going to hurt me. He wasn't Jeff.

"You were having a bad dream," I said in answer to his silent stare.

"No, I wasn't." Duke looked at where he grasped my wrist. His lips pursed, and he quickly let go. "I'm sorry. Did I hurt you?"

"You didn't. It's okay. I'm sorry I woke you. I'll let you get back to sleep." I sighed, not wanting to leave, and pushed off the bed. Duke reached out to grab my hand before I took a step, halting me.

"Stay?" Duke's voice croaked. I think he was just as surprised by the request as I was.

"What?" Too many emotions streaked across his face,

so fast it was hard to identify just one. I wanted to feather my fingers across the deep grooves of his forehead. His eyes slammed shut, and his jaw clenched tightly. I stayed quiet, not wanting to interrupt the internal battle he seemed to be fighting. His throat bobbed as he forced himself to swallow before he took a deep breath.

"Will you stay with me a little longer?" His deep baritone was laced with sleep and a hint of vulnerability. My heart ached to do whatever I could do to help him.

"Of course." I sat on the mattress, and Duke scooted over to make room for me. He turned on his side, facing my direction, and I inched farther onto the bed. "Are you sure you're okay?"

"Yes." His reply was soft and low as his eyes shut. His hand reached for mine. I loved the heat of his touch and how his callused fingers held mine tight.

I studied him as his breathing evened out and his face slackened. He looked so peaceful now. When I thought he was in a deep enough sleep, I shifted to leave, but Duke's arm wrapped around my waist. His eyes were still closed, and his even breathing told me he was still asleep. With a light grunt, he tugged me closer, and I let go of any resistance. Duke pulled me in tight and spooned me from behind. He gave a sigh, and his muscles relaxed into my back. He was asleep and content. And I was in his arms.

My body heated as I realized both of us were half naked, and as much as I desired him, I wanted to comfort him so much more. I wanted to fall asleep with him and not just for tonight.

I took a deep breath, my nose buried in his pillow, relishing the scent of pine that tickled my nose. It had been a long time since I'd slept in someone's arms. Jeff didn't like me on his side of the bed after the first year we'd moved in together. There was no cuddling in our relationship. I missed the closeness of a person and the tenderness of the contact. My eyes grew heavy, and it wasn't long before I drifted to sleep.

When I woke the next morning, Duke was gone. His side of the bed was cold. It wasn't like I'd expected something to come out of last night, but I still had to fight the feeling of rejection.

DUKE

*M*y internal alarm had me waking before the sun came up, as usual. But the warm body pressed against my front kept me calmer than I typically was in the mornings. I breathed in the scent of vanilla and strawberries, savoring the moment before I had to give it up. I opened my eyes to Abbey tucked into me, still fast asleep.

The memories from the night before hit me. I'd had another nightmare. After not having one for two days, I'd let my guard down and a bad one slipped in.

I remembered waking up to find Abbey with me. She was worried about me, which meant I'd had a bad enough dream that I woke her. Images of my last fight overseas seeped into my head. I'd dreamed about my brothers being killed in the ambush and me barely making it out alive.

As I shifted, Abbey whimpered. Instinctively, I leaned over and pressed my lips to her forehead. In a moment of weakness, I'd asked her to stay, and she had. This beautiful woman was an angel. But I couldn't stay in bed with her. I didn't want to give her the wrong idea. As much as I would love to find a woman, to find someone who would accept my damaged and broken soul... it was impossible to hope for.

Jax was at the door waiting for me and our morning run. He sat up as I extracted myself from the sheet, and I noticed a blanket draped over Abbey. I didn't remember doing that, nor did I recall her having it in the middle of the night. It must have been Liam.

The border collie waited patiently for me to grab my running clothes and change in the hallway. We ran our usual route, and when we returned, Liam was in the kitchen making coffee.

"Have another episode last night?" Liam handed me a cup of steaming hot liquid.

"What makes you think that?" I mumbled, letting the coffee work its way through my veins.

"I was on my way to check on you when I saw Abbey go into your room. She's gotten to you, hasn't she?" He smirked behind his cup. "You like her."

I grunted. "Why would you even think that?"

"Because you wouldn't have let her in your bed otherwise." Liam turned to leave the kitchen. At the doorway, he stopped. "A tip, some insight if you will... next time, let her under the covers. That way, she can feel how much she affects you in the morning."

I groaned at Liam's retreating chuckle. That was all I needed. A mental image of waking up with Abbey's naked body pressed against me. I adjusted my hardening cock.

Fucking Liam. The asshole knew what buttons to push and when.

I needed to shower and calm myself before she woke up, or I was going to be in trouble.

I glanced in my room to see if Abbey was still asleep before going to the guest bathroom. I didn't want to wake her by showering in my room, but the bed was empty. My stomach twisted at the loss of her in my personal space, of not seeing her in her little tank and underwear again. I groaned. This was not helping.

Shoving that thought away, I stripped out of my sweaty clothes and headed for the bathroom. The cold water did nothing to alleviate my intense need for her. I grunted, fisted my cock, and pulled up images of Abbey in nothing but my t-shirt. The way it hung off her body, exposing her creamy skin, like it wanted me to touch it. I pumped my cock faster, imagining her toned legs wrapped around me as she rode my cock. My cum came in thick ropes as I moaned her name. It had been too long since I'd had a release, let alone one inside a woman, but it would have to do.

When I entered the kitchen, dressed and ready to go to town, Abbey was sitting at the counter, sipping her coffee. She looked up from her phone and smiled.

"Morning." I poured my second cup.

"Good morning." She smiled.

The tension in my shoulders released. She wasn't going to try to talk about last night. "We can go to town this morning and pick up your car. Chase said it was ready to go. He looked over everything, and it should be as good as new."

"Great. Thank you. I was afraid I ruined it by running out of gas." She let out a deep sigh.

"Not ruin…" My eyebrows scrunched, and I looked directly into her eyes. "But you need to make sure you don't do that again. It'll kill your engine," I said, a little too sternly, even for my liking. I didn't want to think about her being stranded anywhere again, and it angered me to think about what might have happened to her if I hadn't come along.

"Yes, sir," she said, lowering her gaze. If it was a different situation, her response would have been hot, but not when she said it in defeat. I brushed away the feeling of unease that settled in my stomach. I hadn't meant for it to sound like I was reprimanding her, but she needed to know the severity of the situation.

"Maybe after, we can see about your phone. There's a store in town that might be able to help you extend the reception." She gave me a weak smile. "We can head out when you're ready."

"Just give me a few minutes to grab my things." Abbey tossed the last of her coffee into the sink and rushed to her room. I couldn't help but sneak a glance at her ass as she dashed down the hall. Her jeans hugged her curves and cupped her cheeks nicely. She was a tiny thing but would still fit nicely in my hands.

Fuck.

I shook my head and chugged the rest of the steaming liquid. I could make it through today without embarrassing myself. Just because she was working her way under my skin didn't mean anything.

When she reappeared, her bag was slung over her

shoulder, and her smile warmed my chest. She seemed to have brushed off my harsh tone from before, but it still seemed like there was more to it than that. Though I wanted to know what it was, I wasn't going to intrude.

The drive to town was pleasant. She told me about how she went to art school and what kinds of things she liked to draw and paint. I told her a little about growing up in town with Jessie, Gavin, and Travis. She asked about my work, and I went into detail about how I was a part-time sheriff for the town and the rest of my time was at the ranch running security. A lot of people thought I was crazy when they learned what I did, but she didn't. Abbey seemed more interested in the nuances of my jobs than being turned off by them.

"Let's reorganize a little. Let's go to the phone store first, then we can grab some lunch in town and pick your car up on the way out. How does that sound?" I stopped at a red light in town.

"Sounds good to me." She radiated excitement as she practically bounced in her seat. Her eyes flit from one shop to the next. "This place is so cute. I'd expected the downtown area to be so tiny, tucked in the middle of nowhere, but it seems so much bigger."

"After a while, it'll start feeling small and suffocating," I mumbled. Cottonwood Creek wasn't for everyone. She glanced my way with her eyebrow arched high, but I shrugged. It wasn't the time to get into that conversation.

At the cellular store, we ended up getting her a tempo-rary phone since she didn't want to change the carrier. The new one she got gave her enough coverage so she had service while she was here visiting, and I felt more comfortable knowing she had a working phone at all times. When we got it activated, I put my phone number in it in case she ever needed anything. A pang of sadness hit me knowing she'd have to leave at some point. I didn't want that.

Our next stop was to the local diner, The Cotton Patch. I hadn't eaten here since I was in high school. We arrived just as the lunch group was leaving, but there were still a good number of patrons lingering, who all happened to glance up when we entered.

Fuck me. I hated the attention.

"Two for lunch today, Duke?" Shelby, the owner's wife, called from behind the counter.

"Yes, ma'am." Shelby and her husband, Wayne, had owned the diner since before I was born. We used to all hang out here growing up, and Jessie even had her first job here.

"Take any open table you'd like." She waved her hand around. "I'll be right with you."

I led Abbey to a corner booth and away from wandering eyes. Most of the town only saw me when I was on duty. I didn't make it a habit to linger off the clock.

"What do you normally get here?" Abbey glanced from the menu on the table. "Everything sounds delicious."

"I don't normally come here." I shrugged.

"You mean you're a cop in this town, and you don't eat lunch here almost every shift?" Abbey tilted her head, the corners of her mouth wrinkled as she fought a smile.

"I usually take the outer zones on shift."

Her eyebrows nearly touched. "What does that mean?"

"I patrol the roads farthest from town."

"That doesn't mean you can't come in for breakfast before a shift or any other meal when you're in town." Abbey's mouth turned down. Before I could reply, Shelby interrupted.

"Can I get you something to drink, dear?" she asked Abbey.

"Sweet tea, please."

"Of course. And a Coke for you, Duke?"

I nodded. After all these years, she still remembered I was addicted to that sugary-sweet, carbonated beverage. Liam constantly made fun of me for it, but it was my one and only vice.

"Do you know what you'd like, or do you need a few more minutes?" Shelby had her pen poised.

"Do you have any recommendations?" Abbey met her gaze.

"Sure, sweetie. Wayne makes a mean burger, but the turkey club is my favorite. The chili is also a winner, but I don't want to brag." Shelby placed her hand on her chest and smiled, making Abbey giggle.

"That all sounds amazing."

"Shall we make it a half turkey club, cup of chili, and some fries?"

Abbey grinned and nodded at the recommendation.

"Cheeseburger with sautéed onions and mushrooms with fries for you?"

Damn, the old woman had a good memory. "Please."

She winked before turning and grabbing our drinks. I downed half my glass the moment she set it in front of me. I needed something to calm my nerves. You could take the boy out of the town, but the town never forgets the boy.

When Shelby returned with a refill, another tiny figure followed close behind.

Kill me now.

"What do you want?" I growled. Abbey glanced at me quickly before smiling at the new arrival.

"Don't be rude, Duke," the tiny sprout of a girl scolded before turning to Abbey. Her size was deceptive. She might be twenty-three, but she was too perceptive for my liking. How I hadn't spotted her when we first walked in was beyond me. "Hi, I'm Lizzy." She gave a tiny wave and a sweet smile to Abbey.

"Hi, Lizzy. I'm Abbey."

"Again, what do you want?" I narrowed my eyes at my little sister.

"I wanted to meet the woman who was able to get my grumpy-ass brother out and socializing." She thumbed in my direction. Of course she was here to get the juicy gossip. That way, she could be the first to spread it around. Being five years younger than me, she was still young and wanted to be involved everywhere.

"Okay, you've met her. Now will you leave us be?" I wanted Abbey all to myself, and I wanted to ignore everyone else in town like I always did.

"Oh, come on, Duke. You never come to town anymore. I hardly see you, and when I finally do, you have a complete stranger with you. How did you get such a cute woman to even agree to go out to lunch with you?" She waggled her eyebrows.

"This is Abbey. She's new to the ranch, and we came to

town to pick up her car from Chase's. Happy?"

"And now defensive." She slowly grinned and turned to Abbey. "So, what do you make of my brother?"

"Umm…" Abbey wrinkled her napkin in her lap. As much as I wanted to know what she thought about me, this was not the time or the way to go about it.

Wait, no. I didn't want to know what she thought about me. I didn't need to know.

"Lizzy," I hissed. "Go away."

She laughed but didn't pull her eyes from Abbey.

"Duke found me the other day with my car broken down. I was on my way to the ranch, and he graciously helped me out. Since he was the one who called for a tow truck to take my car, he was the one who volunteered to help me retrieve it. He's been very sweet and caring since I met him. I would've been lost without him and probably still stranded." Abbey's eyes held mine as she said the last part, and my heart pounded in my chest.

"Ahh, that's so sweet. Well, don't let this jerk scare you away. He barely comes to town ever since he returned home all those years ago. The hero won't grace us with his presence. But if you like him, he is a keeper." She eyed me, knowing full well she was overstepping. This was why I avoided town, so no one could be in my business. Especially my family.

"Lizzy…" I warned.

"Okay, I'll leave you two alone. Make sure to call Mom. You know she'll freak when she hears you were in town and didn't stop by." Lizzy threw up her hands and slowly retreated to her booth of friends.

When Lizzy was out of earshot, Abbey leaned in and

69

whispered, "Why did she call you a hero?"

"I'd rather not talk about it right now," I grunted.

She nodded solemnly. I didn't want to sound like an asshole, but this wasn't really the place to have a heart to heart. The less she knew, the better off she was. She couldn't judge me or think any less of me if she didn't know.

"Tell me about your family." She didn't need to know about mine, but I was curious about hers. I wanted to continue our easy conversation from the ride to town.

"There's not much to tell. My father died when I was little. My mother worked hard to provide for us. She now has a new boyfriend who is great for her. I don't have any siblings besides Blake and Grace. We all grew up together, and I consider them my sisters," Abbey started, and we flowed into our casual conversation.

It didn't take long for our meals to arrive, and we dug in. The burger tasted just as I remembered, and Abbey raved over her lunch.

When we piled into my SUV, Abbey turned in her seat and stared at me.

"What?"

"Can you tell me now?" she asked in a soft, soothing tone.

"Tell you what?" I had hoped she would drop it, but she hadn't.

"Tell me why people were so surprised to see you today. Why you don't want to come to town?"

I sighed and looked out the window, surprised at how much I wanted to tell her the truth. "Because I don't want people to see how broken I am. When I'm working, I have a focus. When I'm not, all I can see are people analyzing my every move."

"How are you broken?"

"It's a long story." I rubbed at the back of my neck, working out how much to say.

"I'm not going anywhere." She scooted closer to me. Not so close we touched, but close enough the heat of her body seared into me.

I sighed. She wasn't going to let this go. "When I graduated, I wanted to get out of here and do something that mattered. Being in this town… it's a dead end. So I left, and I joined the military. During my last tour, my team walked into an ambush. Only two of us came out of it alive." My throat tightened, and I couldn't continue any farther. My vision tunneled and blurred out completely. It felt impossible to catch a breath.

"Duke?" Everything muffled around me.

A warm presence touched my forearm. It stayed there as the comfort of it seeped into my arm and then throughout my body as a calmness washed over me.

"Duke, come back to me. Everything's going to be okay. Just look at me."

The warmth stayed in my arm and also appeared against my cheek, and everything slowly cleared. Abbey's thumb rubbed back and forth, pulling me out of my waking nightmare. When I lifted my eyes, she held me in her gaze. Her other hand rested on my arm, her fingers caressing my skin.

"There you are."

Her soft voice washed over me, and I took a deep breath.

ABBEY

"There you are." I stroked Duke's cheek. When he was telling me about his tour, he'd suddenly stopped and froze. His eyes clouded over, and his breathing became erratic. He was having a panic attack, and I couldn't bear to see him like that.

It took a few minutes before I could bring him to focus. When I touched him, it helped. And then when I laid my hand on his face and stroked his cheek, he came out of it completely.

He let out a deep breath and cupped my hand to his cheek. I liked the way his scruff scratched against my palm.

"Hi," I breathed. "You're back."

"Sorry," his voice caught.

"It's okay." I moved my thumb along his cheekbone, soft and slow.

Duke held my hand a moment longer before pulling away. I let my hand drop and placed it in my lap along with my other. He was retreating, and I didn't know him well enough to push him to accept my comfort any further than I already had.

This was the second time I'd seen him vulnerable, and he pulled away from me as soon as it was over. He only needed me in the moment, and I knew well enough not to assume I was making that much of a difference for him. He didn't need me. I was sure he would have handled his nightmare all by himself, and if I hadn't asked questions, he wouldn't have had this episode at all.

"Thank you."

I almost missed his words. He'd spoken them so quietly.

When I met his eyes, there was only sincerity. "Of course." I couldn't keep his gaze. Instead, I twisted my hands in my lap and glanced out the window. "What next?"

"We have your phone taken care of and lunch, so that means your car. Let's get it and head to the ranch. I don't want to be here too long and end up driving in the dark."

I snort-laughed. "Duke, it's two-thirty. The sun doesn't set for hours."

"And people around here will keep you tied up for hours with their curiosity. You're the new person in town. Everyone wants to know all about you. If we don't get out of here soon, the whole town will mob the repair shop." His face scrunched and frustration filled his eyes.

I couldn't help but laugh at the horror reflected in his expression. Just like him, I wasn't interested in being the center of attention today. Just like him, I wasn't ready to tell my story to a bunch of strangers.

But I needed to know one thing before we left. I

pulled on a straight face and asked, "Are you good, or do you need me to drive?" I already knew the answer, but I wanted to see how he'd react. Any man would snap out of whatever they were thinking, come back to their senses, and go all caveman about their car.

He pointed his finger at me. "You are not driving my patrol car, but maybe you can have a go at my truck back at the ranch." He smiled, and I felt my heart flutter. The grin made him look so much younger and even more handsome. His answer was not what I had expected, but now I had butterflies in my stomach.

The mechanic's shop was only a few minutes down the road. When we arrived, the place was empty except for the handsome guy around my age behind the counter. I swear there was something in the water around here. We approached the counter, and he smiled at me. It was pleasant, but nothing compared to when Duke or Liam smiled at me. They turned my insides upside down.

"Chase," Duke greeted the man with a head nod.

"Hey, Duke. You here to pick up the car?" Chase reached under the counter and produced a folder. He took out a few forms.

"Yes. This is Abbey. It's her car. What do you need from her in order to release it?" Duke glanced at me, and I stepped forward and extended my hand.

"Nice to meet you, Abbey. I'm Chase." He gave me a firm shake and then dropped my hand.

"Is this your shop?" I looked around. It was clean and more maintained than I would have expected for a small-town mechanic. Movies usually depicted them as dirty and unkempt, but Chase's shop was anything but.

"It is. I've had it for a few years now. I bought it from the original owner and changed it up a bit."

"Wow, that's incredible. What do you need from me?" My innate curiosity about people wanted to know how someone so young would have been able to buy out the owner, but I knew we were tight on time. Duke wanted to get home, and I was ready to get back to the ranch as well.

"Just fill out this form here. Just some basic information. While you do that, I'll bring the car around." He turned the form to me, and I grabbed the pen from the counter to complete the information.

"How much do I owe you? Was there anything else wrong with it that needed fixing?" I'd hoped it wasn't too much. I didn't have a lot saved up, especially since most of my money was in an account controlled by Jeff, but I did have an emergency credit card I could put it on.

"No charge. Anything for my friend Officer Bennett. And your car was fine. It's old and needed some basic maintenance. I did an oil change and topped off some fluids. I changed your air filter too since it's a bit dustier around here than Georgia."

My eyebrows pushed together. That didn't sound right. "Are you sure?" Why did I have a feeling he might have done more? My car hadn't been running all that great, even when it did have gas.

He nodded. "I'll be right back with the car." Chase disappeared out back.

"What's wrong?" Duke appeared next to me, his eyes narrowed. I loved and hated how quickly he was learning my moods.

"It feels weird not paying him anything. I've never

gotten anything for free before." I tucked my hair behind my ear.

He chuckled. "You might need to get used to that around here." His arm bumped my shoulder, and I could see he was fighting a smile.

Chase pulled my beat-up little car around to the front just as we exited. I barely recognized it. It was shiny and clean.

"You washed it?" I lifted my eyebrows. I also had a sneaking suspicion he detailed the inside too.

Chase shrugged. "Every car gets it when they come through right now. My nephew does it. He's trying to save up for a new saddle." The smile of pride at the mention of his nephew melted my heart.

"Well, then, please give my compliments to him and make sure he gets this." I handed Chase a twenty from my purse. He beamed, and I couldn't help but smile back. He clearly loved his nephew, and I thought it was sweet he gave him an opportunity to earn money at the shop. I glanced at Duke. I was still suspicious about why there was no charge for the work on my car. I had a sneaking suspicion Duke had something to do with it with the way Chase said Officer Bennett.

Chase nodded to me and then to Duke before disappearing into his shop. I stood in the open door, staring up at Duke, wondering if I should ask him point-blank. Before I could decide, my breath caught as Duke caged me in. He was close but not so close that he made me nervous. His body blocked the sun like he had done the first time we'd met. I bit my lip, my emotions rioting in my stomach the longer he stared at me. I drew in a deep breath, his scent surrounding me. He pinched my chin with his thumb and forefinger, and butterflies erupted in my stomach.

"Follow me to the ranch. I'll be watching closely, but if something goes wrong, honk at me. You also have my cell, but I'd rather you not talk and drive. Be mindful of animals. They tend to come out of nowhere around here." His steady gaze pinned me in place, and my body heated from head to toe.

"Yes, sir," I whispered.

A low growl left his lips, and my skin tingled. He may be grumpy, but he was also protective and demanding. It must be how he showed he cared, and realizing that made me want to yank his head down and kiss him.

He leaned in closer, then paused.

Emotions flashed one by one in his eyes as our gazes locked together. Anger, sorrow, need, and what I hoped was lust were the ones I could make out.

I licked my parched lips. He was only inches from me, and the tension rolled off him in waves. I leaned in, and my eyes fluttered closed.

His hand dropped from my face, and I took a second before opening my eyes to hide the hurt from his rejection. I hated that he'd pulled away. Although, without him so close, reality crept in. His distance was for the best. He told me why he thought he was too broken, but the kicker was, he had no idea how broken I was too.

I hurriedly got behind the wheel of my car and shut the door. He lingered outside for a moment, making sure I'd started the car before he headed to his patrol car. Fiddling with the radio, I found a clear station with decent music to keep me occupied on the drive. It had been nice having Duke to talk to on the way into town. The longer I drove, the more I felt like when I had arrived a few days ago—alone and falling apart, with nowhere to go.

Needing the distraction, I called my mom to let her know where I was.

"Hello," she answered tentatively on the third ring, and I realized she wouldn't recognize this number.

"Hi, Mom. It's me, Abbey." I tried to sound cheerful. I wasn't ready to tell her about Jeff.

"Oh, Abbey. I didn't recognize your number. Did you get a new one?" Now that she knew it was me, I could hear the joy in her voice.

"Only a temporary one. That's why I'm calling. I wanted to let you know that I ended up not going home. I made a detour to visit Blake and Grace in Texas. My cell doesn't work out here, so I just popped into town and got a temp one."

"Oh, honey, that's great. I'm so glad you're seeing the girls. It's been so long."

"I know. And I didn't want you to be worried if you tried to call me and I wasn't answering. So, this is my new phone for now, in case you need me."

"How long are you staying?" Her voice was full of excitement. She'd been pushing me to go visit the girls since they landed here, but I couldn't tell her Jeff never allowed me to.

"I'm not sure yet. At least a few more days."

There was a rustling on the other end of the phone. She was speaking to someone, likely her boyfriend, but I couldn't make out what she was saying. "I'm so happy you're out and about. Have fun and give the girls my love. I've got to go. I love you."

"Okay, Mom. Love you too. Bye." I disconnected the call and stared at the back end of Duke's SUV.

That was easier than I'd thought. I hadn't anticipated a full-on interrogation, but I thought she would be more curious. She probably expected I had Jeff with me and everything was going well.

The rest of the drive was uneventful. My old beat-up car ran better than it had in years, making me think Chase did more than he let on. When we pulled up, Liam was waiting outside.

"How was it?" he asked when he opened my door to help me out.

Duke had disappeared into the house the second we arrived. I tried my best to cover the hurt feelings that surfaced. He hadn't even checked in with me when we pulled in after being so worried about me following him. He was hot and cold. Case in point, he'd just vanished without a word.

Liam caught my gaze lingering on the front entryway. "Don't mind him. He's always in a bit of a mood when he comes back from town. Too many people, too many questions."

I smiled. "It was fine. I got a temporary phone, we had lunch, and then we got my car." Liam took my bag and slung it over his shoulder before resting his hand on my lower back and steering me toward the house.

"At least you made it back before dark," he said with a smile.

"Why is everyone so worried about driving in the dark around here?"

"There are no lights and animals run into the road. It can get very dangerous." He stopped and stood directly in front of me. "Deer pop out of nowhere, and you could end up in a ditch or wrapped around a tree. Abbey, please don't drive at night around here," Liam pleaded.

"I don't have any intentions of driving anywhere at night." Why would I when everything I needed was right here?

Liam let out a deep breath. "Good. The girls are waiting for you inside."

I squeaked, dancing in place. I could get used to seeing them all the time. I'd missed them so much.

"Go inside, *dulcinée,* I've got your bag."

"What does that mean, dulcinée?"

"I'll tell you another time. You don't want to keep the girls waiting." He nudged me to door, and I ran inside, excited to see them.

LIAM

I wouldn't admit it to anyone, but I had missed Abbey's warm presence in the house when Duke had taken her to town. It didn't matter they were only gone for a few hours. I'd wanted to go with them but didn't want to overwhelm her.

One look at her, and I knew Abbey was going to be special to us, but I needed Duke to see it. He thought he was too broken for anyone, even though he had openly invited her to stay with us and took her to town. Not to mention, he invited her into his bed. He might not be able to see what she did to him, but I could.

It didn't help the twinge of jealousy pitted in my stomach. I'd let the grumpy bastard have all day with her. Then the girls showed up and said they were taking her.

When I entered the house, I could hear the girls laughing. They were in Abbey's room, no doubt. Didn't matter how old you were, girl time was girl time.

Duke was on the couch, flipping through channels on the TV. "Did everything go well in town?"

He huffed, "It's never good when I go to town."

"So you say." I plopped in my spot and watched as he went back and forth, never landing on something to watch. "You're making me dizzy. Will you just pick something to watch?"

"There's nothing good on." He tossed the remote onto the cushion beside him.

"It's Sunday, Duke. Find a game." Something was *definitely* going on with him. There was always some sporting game on TV on Sundays.

"Right." Duke returned to flipping through the channels until he found a game he liked. "I forgot what day it was."

"What happened in town?" I looked closer at his body language—the stiff set of his shoulders, the restless tapping of his foot. "What are you not telling me?"

"I almost kissed her." He didn't elaborate.

"You can't just say that and not tell me what happened. Why *didn't* you kiss her?" I threw my hands up.

"She helped me out in town today. The memories overwhelmed me, and she helped bring me back. I got caught up in the moment, but I didn't kiss her because she doesn't need someone like me screwing up her life." He ran a hand down his face.

"Whatever happened to our agreement that we would at least try to find someone for us? Did you forget all about it? It's been years, and I've stood by and let you take the lead. Let you decide when you were ready. Find the girl who speaks to you. Well, I think we've found her, and you run and hide." I tried to keep my voice down so the girls couldn't hear us, but Duke was being ridiculous. "I'm done waiting, Duke."

He turned the TV up. If he hadn't become my best friend in the ten years we'd known each other, I would have left him a long time ago. He needed me, and as much as I hated to admit it, I needed him just as much.

Without anyone around, I felt alone and helpless. Without a purpose. Even being on a team didn't help when you couldn't get close to anyone because no one stayed long enough. Blake and Grace were different. I took them under my wing, and they became family.

At least on the Kingston team, I could stay as long as I wanted. Here I had a place to call home, and they needed me in the beginning when they were building their team.

Then I met Duke, and everything solidified. He was someone I could look after and help. He was the brother I never got to have. We balanced each other out.

And after being introduced to the Cosland relationships the Kingstons brought with them, Duke was someone I trusted enough to share a woman with. He could protect and love her while I was away.

Maybe it was time for me to take charge and have him fall in line. I didn't want Abbey to slip away, not when we could be so close to love.

A door opened in the hall, and the thudding of feet grew louder as the girls emerged from the room and headed toward us.

"We're taking Abbey tonight for dinner." Grace settled on the arm of the couch next to me.

"Who's playing?" Abbey asked, stepping behind the

couch and resting her hands on the back between Duke and me.

"Ravens versus Lions," Duke mumbled.

"Eh, at least I won't be missing much," Abbey said, and Duke glanced at her. "Who plays tonight?"

"Saints versus Patriots," Duke answered.

"Oooh, that should be a good game." Abbey rubbed her hands together.

"Do I even want to know which team you favor?" Duke grumbled, and I saw the tilt of a smile at the corner of his lips.

"Nope," she said and tapped him on the nose. His eyes widened, and I stifled a laugh.

"Let's go, let's go, let's go. I'm hungry." Blake's patience wore thinner every day.

"You're always hungry," I commented, earning a smack to the back of my head from Grace.

"What's for dinner tonight?" I asked.

"Chicken parmesan, Caesar salad, garlic rolls, and I think Jessie also mentioned baked ziti too. Italian night." Blake wiggled in her spot.

"Sounds like we're having dinner with everyone tonight." I looked at Duke, and he grunted in reply. "Maybe we'll see you ladies there in a bit." I patted Grace's leg, and she stood from her perch.

"See you then." Abbey's hand grazed the back of my neck as she slid it along the top of the couch, following the girls out the door. It wasn't until the front door was shut that I could peel my eyes away from where Abbey had disappeared.

"Would food make you feel better?" I arched an eyebrow at Duke.

He shrugged. "We went to The Cotton Patch for lunch, but I could still eat."

"I'm going to take a shower. We can leave in thirty. That way, you can continue to pretend you didn't want to join them for dinner, and we can eat by ourselves." I smirked.

I got up and headed for the shower. I'd spent a long day in the barn, checking on Zeus and doing exercises to see if we could start training again. Caleb, our resident equine vet, and Alex, our previous vet and the Kingstons' fiancé, had given us the go ahead to start, but I wanted to make sure he was ready too. After the grueling Olympics only a few months ago, I wasn't in a rush to put the pressure on him.

Passing by Abbey's room, I noticed she had left the door half open. Not wanting Jax to get into her things, I went to close the door and paused. Her notepad on the nearby nightstand caught my eye. I knew it was wrong to look at her things, but the closer I got to it, I realized it was a drawing of Zeus. I was amazed at the details.

She made him look so lifelike. He was just as noble and stunning in this picture as he was in person. The lines and shadows perfectly depicted him, and I wanted nothing more than to keep this picture for myself. I only wished I had drawings like this of my horses I'd had growing up.

I turned the page in the book, and Jax's silly face greeted me. I laughed at the tongue hanging out, just like he always did when he was happy. The next page was one of a landscape, and it looked remarkably like the pasture I'd found her in. It didn't look like she'd finished it yet, and I wondered if we picnicked there if she might find inspiration again.

When I flipped to the next page, my heart nearly stopped.

It was a picture of Duke.

She'd captured him in his uniform. His face was serious, like always. Next was a picture of Duke on the couch. This must have been when they were watching the game together. Her memory was incredible to draw these after the fact. The next one caught me by surprise. She'd drawn Duke shirtless, in bed with his sheet around his waist. These pictures of Duke had my hopes up that she liked him.

I had to wonder, if I flipped again, would there be a picture of me in here?

I chanced the disappointment and kept going. My breath caught at the sight of me on the next page. It was the morning I woke her when the girls arrived. I hadn't realized how much she'd paid attention to that moment. I had hooded eyes that flared with a need I could remember all too well. My arm was raised to rest on the casing above the door. Her quick strokes had captured each muscle in my body, which tightened, mimicking the drawing as I remembered seeing her in her panties and tank. Her breasts spilled over the top and her hair was tousled from sleep, but I imagined that's how it looked after sex, spread across her pillow.

My dick awakened at the memory of her creamy toned legs, the swells of her breasts, and her tiny waist.

She was so much smaller than me, I kept imaging what it would be like to hoist her against the wall. My pants were growing tighter with every second. I needed to cool down before I went to dinner.

As much as I wanted to rush through my shower, I stayed in a few minutes longer and let the spray wash away my cum that streaked the tile and wall. I grabbed a fresh shirt and jeans from my dresser and met Duke in the living room, on the couch, right where I'd left him.

I wanted to tell him about the sketches, but I didn't want to freak him out more than he already was. He liked Abbey, but he didn't want to admit it. If he knew there was a possibility she liked him, too, he would retreat even further.

"Let's go, *connard*." I smacked Duke on the shoulder. It was the last quarter of the game, but I knew this wasn't one he particularly cared about. He was a die-hard Cowboys fan, and they didn't play until Monday night.

"We have leftovers in the fridge. I'll just eat that. You go on ahead." He pretended to be glued to the game.

"Fuck that. Get off your ass, Duke, and come with me. Stop hiding, or I will tell Jessie you are in here sulking instead of eating one of your favorite meals. Do you want to hurt her feelings?" His face snapped to mine, and he narrowed his eyes. I was serious, and he knew it.

He marched to the door. With any luck, he'd be more pleasant with some food in him. I didn't want him scaring Abbey away.

The dining hall was packed when we got there. I immediately scanned the crowd for Abbey and the girls, spotting them near the far end. It didn't look like there

87

were any free seats nearby, so we'd have to keep an eye on her from afar. By the time we grabbed our plates, a couple spots across from Gavin and Travis opened up. We could see Abbey over their shoulders the whole time. We eased into their conversation.

"How was town?" Gavin asked Duke, who grunted his response with a shoulder shrug. "That bad?"

"I thought you went to grab Abbey's car?" Travis pointed his fork at Duke.

"And got her a phone and went to lunch," Duke said between bites.

Gavin and Travis exchanged a look. "You took her out to lunch?" Gavin asked.

"In town?" Travis finished the question. It was weird sometimes when they did that. They did that with Duke too, but I assumed it was what happened when you literally grew up with someone since you could talk. "The Cotton Patch?"

Duke nodded.

I glanced over Gavin's shoulder to see Abbey laughing at something. She tucked her hair behind her ear and sipped her water. The way her lips wrapped around her straw had my cock pulsing, and the image of her lips on my body had me clenching my fist.

"Is it time for the two of you to fall?" Travis chuckled, following my gaze.

My eyes snapped to his. "Fall?"

"You can't stop looking at her. Duke took the girl to lunch, and don't think I haven't noticed your eyes popping over to her too." Travis circled his finger at Duke. "You two have it bad for her."

I shrugged. "I won't deny it, but he wants to pussyfoot around the idea."

Duke gave me the middle finger, and we all laughed. Even Duke. Barely.

A smile graced his face. Then his gaze lingered over Travis' shoulder before he let out a long breath. "She deserves better than me."

"Duke, how many times do we have to tell you? You deserve to be happy. You can't let what happened to you define the rest of your life. If this is what you want, you should go for it."

I sent a silent thank you to Gavin for his much-needed words. If anyone could talk some reason into Duke, it was Gavin. Plus, he and Travis had fallen first out of everyone. And now they were happily in love with Blake and expanding their family.

I took a quick peek at Abbey again to see her looking toward us. When she saw me, she smiled and went back to her conversation with the girls. I would have bet anything her cheeks were a rosy color, but the lighting in here was horrendous.

After I convinced Duke to open and give love a shot, I was going to discover all the ways I could make her blush.

ABBEY

"Those boys haven't taken their eyes off you since they walked in." Grace nudged me.

"What? That can't be true." I glanced at their table, and sure enough, Liam was staring in my direction. My cheeks heated as I smiled.

"Believe me now?" Grace laughed.

"I think you're exaggerating. It was only Liam." I pursed my lips, afraid I'd say how much I wanted *both* of them not to be able to take their eyes off me.

"Oh, Duke was laser focused on you the moment he stepped foot in the dining hall," Jessie chimed in.

I shook my head. She had to be mistaken. There was no way Duke, of all people, looked at me like that.

"Those two want you bad," Jessie tilted her head in the guys' direction. She'd walked away from the kitchen to join us while we ate. Her husbands were leaving when we'd arrived, and it was like a punch in the gut watching the two men dote on her and love on her. They looked at her like she hung the moon.

Why wasn't I that lucky?

Jeff treated me well enough in high school, but once we graduated, he stopped spending time with me, or finding special ways to show he cared, and while it wasn't everything, he stopped giving me gifts and taking me out on dates. What hurt even worse was I wasn't good enough to meet his new friends and coworkers, and any time I suggested we get together with them, I was shot down.

What I wouldn't give to be treated like one of the girls here. Their men cherished them completely. It was hard to admit that I was actually jealous of my two best friends. For so long, I'd thought I'd had it all. The long-term boyfriend, the apartment in town, the stay-at-home life. But I was wrong. I realized everything I had was like nothing I wanted.

"Well, that's not going to happen. Remember what happened with my last relationship? I'm not sure I'm ready for anything yet." I propped my elbows on the table and rested my chin on my hand. "As much as I'd really love to, Officer Sexypants over there doesn't want anything to do with me. I don't know why I haven't moved to the bunkhouse yet."

Blake choked on her garlic bread. "Excuse me, did you call Duke Officer Sexypants?"

Shit.

"No." I nearly burst into flames. I hadn't meant to let that slip. The girls squealed, drawing all eyes to our table. I narrowed my gaze, and their squeals turned to laughter. "You guys are impossible."

"Oh, come on, Abbey. You need to loosen up." Grace

laid her hand on mine. I blew out a breath.

"I think you guys need to get your heads checked. There is no way they would go for me if they knew the truth. No one wants someone who can't even keep her ex happy. If wasn't good enough for him, what makes you think I'd be good enough for both of them?" I took a sip of water to hide my watery eyes. They might think it was fun teasing me about Duke and Liam, but it broke my heart knowing I did like them but would never be good enough for them. Duke deserved someone who wasn't broken like me to help him through his pain.

"Abbey, don't you ever think that again. You are not sloppy seconds. You are a beautiful young woman with amazing talent and an awesome personality. Jeff didn't see that, and that was his loss. Now you can find someone who will appreciate you and show you all the love in the world." Leave it to Blake to make me cry. I let a few tears slide down my cheeks before I swiped them away and straightened my spine. If she believed that, then why couldn't I?

Footsteps echoed around us, and suddenly our table was surrounded by tall men. "Come on, ladies, time to go home." Gavin extended a hand to Blake. I pouted and looked from Blake to Grace. It hadn't been nearly long enough to be considered girl time.

"Really? It's so early." Grace whined, then yelped when Scott gave her ass a firm swat.

I laughed along with Jessie as we watched the girls leave with their escorts. Their men were eager for my friends, and who was I to stop them from having a good time?

"You ready to go, Abbey?" I nearly jumped out of my seat at Liam's voice behind me. I hadn't seen him get up from their table.

"Sure," I said once the initial shock wore off. "But what about you, Jessie? Do you want me to wait here with you?"

"Oh no, girl. I'll still be here for another hour or so. One of my men will be here soon to help me and take me home." She waved her arms, shooing me out. "Now, get out of here and go home with these boys."

Before I could respond, Jessie was out of her seat, and I was left looking at a brooding Duke and a smiling Liam. My chest tightened at the sight of them towering over me. It would have been intimidating if they weren't so handsome and made me feel safe in their presence.

Duke extended his hand to me. "Shall we?"

I blinked in surprise. "Okay." I lay my hand in his and felt that same electricity surge through my body. For as much of a fight as I put up with the girls, these two had me weak in the knees every time they looked at me.

AFTER DUKE and Liam walked me to the house, I hid away in my room for the rest of the night. I hadn't wanted to, but I also didn't know how I'd be able to sit on the couch with them all night with the conversation from dinner playing over and over in my head. I tried not to let the girls' words get to me, but it would have been painful sitting between them, knowing I was developing feelings for them and not knowing if they felt the same way.

In my room, I let my imagination run wild. My pencil slid across the paper, capturing the five-o'clock shadow on Liam's chin. I didn't have many of him, and I wanted to change that. There were pictures online I used for inspiration—I may have made the team shirt a little tighter than it actually was, but I didn't want to assume how he looked without it. For a true shirtless sketch, I wanted a firsthand shot to capture the moment. When I drifted to sleep, my night was consumed with dreams starring those two sexy men.

For most of the next day, I went out to the same paddock I'd been in before and tried to finish the landscape, but my mind kept drifting to Duke and Liam. Duke hadn't woken me up last night with a nightmare, and Liam wasn't in the kitchen this morning when I had a cup of coffee.

Were they avoiding me? Were they mad I didn't hang out with them last night? I hated second guessing everything. Maybe my experience with Jeff wasn't a one off, and maybe they were tired of me already.

By the time lunch rolled around, it was too hot for me to stay outside any longer. I hurried to the house as quickly as I could, with Jax right by my side. I desperately wanted a shower after I had a bite to eat. There were still leftovers from taco night the guys said I could have for lunch. The thought instantly made my fingers itch to sketch Liam. I'd done one of him prepping food, but I hadn't paid enough attention that night and the details were off. I grinned. Maybe I could imagine him shirtless with an apron on. Now that would be a drawing I'd take out time after time to look at.

When I reached the house, Liam was on the couch in the living room reading a book.

"I see you have a habit of stealing my dog." Liam didn't look up from his paperback.

"I'm sorry. He just kind of follows me," I whispered, afraid I'd made him angry at me.

He tilted his book and glanced at me over the top.

I sucked in a breath when I saw his face. He was wearing glasses. Why did I just now realize I had a thing for a guy in glasses?

"It's fine. I'm just kidding. It's good he found someone to spend his days with. Otherwise, he'd be running around this place, causing all kinds of trouble." He chuckled.

"Are you sure you don't mind? I can do my best to sneak out without him." I honestly hated the idea. I loved having Jax by my side, but I didn't want Liam angry.

"*Dulcinée*, it's fine. As long as he isn't bothering you." I had no clue what *dulcinée* meant, but he kept calling me it, and I liked it. Not because it was French, but because it seemed like it was just for me. It sounded like an endearment, but I was afraid to ask the meaning again and shatter the sweet thoughts I had about it.

"Okay. Well, I'm going to heat some tacos, and then take a shower. Do you want any?"

"No, but thank you for asking. Enjoy your tacos and your shower." He looked at his book.

If the warmth spreading throughout my chest, face, and ears was any indication, I was turning bright red at him mentioning enjoying a shower. Why did I tell him I was going to do that?

After heating two tacos, I took a quick shower, feeling refreshed and satisfied. I wandered into the living room to discover Liam fully stretched out on the couch, fast asleep. His book had fallen on his chest and his glasses were still perched on his face. He looked so handsome and sweet while asleep.

I hurried to my room and retrieved my sketchbook. I had to capture him in this moment. As soon as my pencil hit the paper, I couldn't stop. He was basically modeling for me. I didn't have to work off a memory or make something up. My hand flew across the page as I captured every line, every curve, every shadow. I lingered on the shading of his lips.

His perfect lips—the ones that smiled and had my panties soaked. They looked so kissable, especially now, all relaxed and slightly parted. I couldn't do that. I couldn't just kiss a guy, could I?

I shook that thought out of my head and continued my shading. The picture was complete, but the itch to draw hadn't eased. I wanted to paint so I could capture all the colors of Liam, but I didn't have that luxury. Although, I could take advantage of having his profile so close to me. I flipped the page and started another of just his face.

My fingers flew fast and furious with each stroke until I had to stop. Something was off. I pursed my lips and tapped the pencil against the page. What was it?

As much as I loved him in his glasses, this sketch demanded a closeup of him without. The way I'd first seen him. Setting my pencil and book down, I carefully extracted the paperback from Liam's hands and put it on the coffee table, making sure to bookmark his page so he could pick up where he left off. Slowly, I removed his glasses and set them down as well.

I was amazed I didn't wake him, but I guess whatever he had done during the morning had exhausted him into a hard nap. My eyes wandered over his face—the face of the man who had been so kind to me, so sweet and patient.

His hair was mussed perfectly except for a stray lock I wanted to fix before beginning my work again. Leaning over him, I swept his dirty-blond hair so it curled slightly over his forehead.

Perfect. Just like him.

My gaze landed on his lips. I'd imagined feeling those lips against mine more times than I could count. I was suddenly aware of how close I had drifted to him. Without thinking, I lightly grazed my lips on his. I felt my skin tingle, and butterflies threatened to erupt from within.

This close, I could smell his cedar soap—the same soap I had in my bathroom but didn't use. I inhaled sharply when I saw Liam's eyes wide open, staring at me.

Oh God. I kissed him. What have I done?

"Oh, no you don't." His words hit me as he grabbed my hands before I could push away. "You can't kiss me and run away."

I tried to stand, but he shot up on the couch and pulled me toward him. Instinctively, I opened my legs as he pulled me on top of his lap to straddle him.

"*Dulcinée, embrasse moi encore,*" Liam whispered.

I drowned in his words, despite not understanding

them. There was no mistaking the desire in his eyes, the way his body tensed as he held himself back, lifting his hand to my face and lightly tracing my lips. He ran the pads of his fingers along my bottom lip, sucking in a breath when my tongue poked out and tasted him. Snaking my hands behind his neck, I pressed my lips to his. He groaned, causing a flutter in my stomach and heat to race to my core.

His mouth slanted over mine, and I reveled in the sparks that flew through my body at such a simple touch. As our kiss deepened, he pulled me in closer; so close, his cock pressed against my clit.

His hand strolled up my spine, and I shivered at the light contact. I pressed my body against his chest.

His tongue flicked across my lips, and I let out a tiny gasp. Liam took the opportunity to slide his tongue past my lips and find mine. Fire consumed me from head to toe and settled between my legs. I'd never felt like this before, and I didn't know what to do. I wanted more. So much more from him.

I rocked my hips forward, grinding on Liam's hard length. His hair wasn't long enough for me to grab, and I was desperate to grab hold of him. Leaving one hand cupped around his neck, I fisted the sleeve of his shirt. Our tongues fought for control, and I let him win. Whatever he wanted to do to me, I'd let him. My desire for him had reached unimaginable heights, and all we'd done was kiss.

His hands squeezed my ass and continued to rock my hips. There were too many clothes between us, and if he didn't let up soon, I had no doubt I'd come from this alone.

A deep growl behind me had me frozen in place.

Duke?

That one sound had me clenching my thighs. Liam gave my lips a light nip and winked before pulling away. His tender smile encouraged me to look over my shoulder.

I turned my head to find Duke near the front door, watching us. His penetrating gaze was locked on Liam and me. His pupils were dilated, and his fists were clenching and unclenching by his side, as though he was stopping himself from running over and joining us.

"I believe Duke wants a sweet kiss from you too," Liam said as he pushed the coffee table farther away with his foot.

This was my dream coming to life. I wanted them both and here was my chance. I bit my bottom lip as I stared at Duke, wondering what he was going to do next.

Liam lifted me from his lap before turning me around to fully face Duke. My breath caught in my throat at the intensity in Duke's gaze. I gave him an encouraging smile, despite the butterflies gathering in my stomach.

Duke stayed firmly planted near the door. His jaw tightened, and a slight tic appeared in his cheek. What if Liam and I had read the situation wrong? What if Duke didn't want to kiss me?

Footsteps thudded across the hardwood. Duke's boots became visible by my feet. My lips parted on a tiny exhale as Duke leaned down, slid his palm to the back of my neck, and crushed his lips to mine. Sighing at how good this felt, I let his tongue slip into my mouth to dance with mine. Needing to touch him, I ran my hand along his stubble and wondered what it would feel like stroking my skin, scratching my inner thighs.

I released him and took a deep breath. "I thought you didn't want me." I ran my tongue along my lower lip, but I couldn't meet his eyes. Each time he'd walked away from me had hurt. I needed to hear him say he wanted me—that this wasn't just in reaction to seeing Liam kissing me, that this wasn't a onetime thing.

"No, darlin'. That was never it." Duke lifted my chin, forcing me to look at him. "You have no idea how much I want you."

"Okay…" I breathed.

"I don't want you to doubt me again." Duke claimed my mouth. Every swipe of his lips felt like a promise. His hands worked their way down my back and gripped my ass, hauling me against him. Tingles raced through my body everywhere we touched. I moaned when his hard cock pressed between us.

"Kiss her neck, Duke. I want to hear those moans loud and clear," Liam ordered, getting up from the couch. His voice was deep with lust, and I wanted to turn around to see him, but Duke held me in his arms. He kissed along my jaw and made his way to my neck.

The brush of his stubble had goosebumps sprouting along my skin. The heat of Liam's body encompassed me from behind before he wrapped his arms around my waist. He pulled me until my ass was pressed against him. I couldn't stop the little wiggle I gave and smiled at the groan he released.

"What do you want, Abbey? Tell us what you want, and we'll give it to you," Duke growled along my neck, sending shivers down my spine.

There was no way he could give me everything I wanted, but maybe I could have something. "I want you. *Both* of you."

"What do you want from us?" Liam ran his tongue up the shell of my ear.

"I want you to make me come." I couldn't believe I'd said it out loud. These two drove me crazy. All I could focus on was their touch, the electric sensations running over my body, and how they lit up every part of me.

"We can do that for you." Liam nipped on my lobe. "Duke, tell me how wet she is." He slid his hands up my stomach and palmed my breasts.

Duke moved his big hands along my stomach until he reached the waistband of my jeans. Unsnapping the button and easing my zipper was slow torture. My hips circled. I wanted his touch on where I needed it the most. I wanted him to feel how wet I was for them.

One hand reached inside, slipping into my panties and carefully avoiding my clit. When he reached my core, I could feel his fingers sliding through my arousal.

"She's soaking," Duke groaned, sending a fresh flood to my aching center. Duke's fingers swirled around my opening.

"Please," I panted.

"When was the last time you had a good orgasm, *dulcinée*?"

"Years," I admitted.

Duke pulled away, his eyebrows furrowed. "How can that be possible?"

"My ex stopped trying a long time ago."

"That will not do. We will make sure you have all the orgasms you want and then some. Enough to make you forget all about your ex." Liam's hands cupped my breasts and pinched my nipples through my bra.

"Yes," I whimpered. That was exactly what I wanted them to do—make me forget all about Jeff and show me what real men were capable of.

"First, you're going to come on Duke's hand. Then on my mouth. And then, if you haven't passed out yet, you'll come on Duke's cock." I liked hearing the demand in Liam's voice, how he took control.

"What about yours?" I wanted both of them.

"What about my what, *dulcinée*?" A smirk lit up his face. He knew exactly what I was asking.

I boldly met his gaze. My days of not asking for what I wanted were over. Being with the two of them brought out a different side of me.

"What about your cock?" I knew I needed his cock inside me, but I wanted him to know I cared as much about his pleasure as he did mine.

"Let's see how you handle three orgasms first. I promise, if I don't get to have you right now, I will be more than happy to wake you up in the morning with my cock buried deep inside you."

"Oh God." I nearly came from his words alone.

Duke leaned forward and bit on my neck at the same time as he pushed a finger into my soaking pussy. I cried out at the combination of sensations. The sharp pain from his teeth and the intrusion of his finger. His palm ground on my clit, and Liam pinched my nipples harder. The pressure inside me was building higher and higher. I was so close already.

I wanted this moment to last forever, but I knew from Liam's words that more pleasure was waiting on the other side of my orgasm.

I let the sensations rush through me, and another pinch, another bite, another rub of Duke's hand, and I was screaming my orgasm right there in the middle of the living room. My knees buckled, and thankfully Liam caught me, hauling me against his body. Duke pulled his hand from my pants, lifted his finger to his mouth, and sucked my desire from it.

He groaned. "Liam, you have to taste her. She's so sweet and delectable."

"I'm trying to decide how I want to eat you, *dulcinée*. I don't know if I want to toss you on the bed and bury my face between your legs or push you against the wall, get down on my knees, and drape your leg over my shoulder."

"Yes, to either or both of those," I mewled at Liam's dirty words.

"Duke, take off her pants," Liam commanded, and I shivered at his tone, wanting him to tell me what to do.

Duke lowered to the coffee table in front of me. Gripping the waistband of my jeans, he worked them down my legs, tapping each foot for me to lift so he could rid me of my pants. His eyes were locked on my underwear. The way they stared at me made me realize the red lace pair was as sexy as I'd hoped it would be.

Duke's eyes slowly met mine. "Fucking hell, darlin'.

These are what you've been wearing? Please tell me the bra matches."

I nodded, biting my lip. The lacy set was a scarlet that popped against my pale skin. Liam's fingers gripped the hem of my shirt, and he stripped it over my head, flinging it to the side.

Liam's chest vibrated against my back, and Duke leaned forward, planting kisses along my stomach. He pulled my panties down my legs and kissed his way to my center.

"Change of plans. I need to eat her out." Duke drew in a deep breath, his fingers digging into my hips. "Then she can come on your cock." Duke stared at me and ran his tongue from my slit upward and flicked my clit, making me gasp. If this was any indication of how attentive these two were, they were going to be the death of me.

DUKE

"*N*ope. You got her first orgasm. This one's mine," Liam growled, turning Abbey to face him. He bent and lifted her into his arms. She wrapped her legs around his hips and held on as he pressed her into the wall.

I followed, not wanting to miss a single second. My mouth watered from the taste of her. I wanted more, but Liam was right. After he gave her an orgasm, then it was fair game. I grabbed her wrists and lifted them above her head, pinning them to the wall. Liam unwrapped her legs from around him and helped her get her footing.

Abbey looked so gorgeous leaning against the wall in nothing but her sexy-as-fuck red bra. The color popped out against her creamy white skin, and I wanted to run my tongue over every curve of her body.

Liam dropped to his knees, kissing his way down her body. He hooked her left leg and threw it over his shoulder. "Are you ready for number two, *dulcinée?*"

He didn't wait for her answer, diving straight in and

burying his face between her thighs. Abbey threw her head back, thumping it against the wall. Her eyes drifted closed, and her mouth hung open in pure ecstasy. My cock strained against the front of my pants at the sight of her pleasure. She took to the two of us so beautifully and seeing her come undone because of us was almost too much for me to handle.

I claimed her mouth, needing to have her. I wanted to tease her soft, lush lips, but my desire had ramped up so much while watching her with Liam that my kiss was firmer than I liked. I started to pull away, but when she followed, I knew she was just as hungry for me as I was for her. Our heads slanted to a better angle while our tongues licked and dueled with each other. I knew by the end of the night, they'd be bruised.

A second later, Abbey gasped into my mouth. Her chin lifted as she rose on her toes. Liam growled and gripped her hips to keep them in place as he feasted on her. The sounds that filled the room made my cock shove painfully against my zipper.

I smiled at Abbey's whimper and trailed kisses along her jaw, down her neck, and over her collarbone. With her hands pinned above her head like they were, it mounded her breasts, making them call out to me, begging to be touched and cherished.

With my free hand, I dipped a finger under the edge of her bra and pulled her nipple out. Then I sucked the perfect thing into my mouth and flicked my tongue over the hard bud. Abbey fought against my hold on her hands.

"Oh God. Don't stop," Abbey cried out, her body trembled.

She was so close. Her hands clenched and twisted, trying to wrap around mine, but I wasn't letting her go. "Do you like Liam licking your sweet pussy?" I nipped at her nipple, making her cry out in need. "Do you want to come, darlin'?"

"Yes, please," she begged. "Don't stop."

Liam groaned, and I could see his hand pumping between her legs. Her hips undulated against Liam's face as she chased her orgasm. If I wasn't careful, I was going to come in my pants.

"Come for us, darlin'. Show us you can handle this." I returned my attention to her nipple. I sucked and licked and nipped until she was writhing in our arms and crying her release. Her fingernails dug into the top of my hand, and I embraced the sting, knowing it was only a result of pleasuring this beautiful creature.

"You were right, Duke. She tastes so sweet. It's irresistible." Liam stood, licked his fingers, and then wiped his mouth with the back of his hand. The shit-eating grin never once left his face.

Abbey sighed and slunk down an inch on the wall. I released her wrists and settled for holding her hips. Her arms wrapped around my neck as she slumped over me. She had to be exhausted from two orgasms, but we weren't done with her yet.

"How are you feeling, darlin'?" I kissed just below her ear.

"That was amazing."

I chuckled at the sound of her dreamy voice. "You ready for more?" The taste of her skin was intoxicating as I licked up her neck and then along her collarbone.

"Only if it means you both get undressed."

"With pleasure." Liam appeared with a glass of water and handed it to Abbey. "Drink, *dulcinée*. You're going to need it. You haven't finished screaming yet." His smile matched mine. I couldn't remember a time when I'd been this happy. It was like Abbey had been with us always. The ease of the three of us together had surprised me. Liam and I had discussed sharing a woman, but this was the first time we'd done so.

Abbey took a big gulp from the cup, and I relieved her of the glass, handing it to Liam. "We need a bed for what I have in mind," I said, bending over and tossing Abbey over my shoulder. Her laughter echoed along the hall as I carried her to Liam's room. His bed was bigger and probably more comfortable than mine.

Abbey's hands gripped my waist, and once I stopped inside Liam's bedroom, she placed a feather-light kiss along my spine.

Carefully, I slid her down my body, keeping her tight against me. Now that we were all on board, I didn't want to be separated from her for long. When I was with her, I felt settled.

With her body pressed against mine, I knew she could feel how hard I was. I loved that she knew how much I wanted her. I unhooked her bra, my eyes tracing each strap as I tugged it over her shoulder, down her arm, and tossed it behind me. My heart pounded in my chest as I took in the perfection of her in front of me. Every inch of her skin beckoned to me, and I wanted to run my tongue over her body.

Abbey reclined on her elbows. *God, she was so sexy.* I

didn't think she even knew just how much her actions turned me on.

I grabbed the back of my shirt, pulling it over my head, and started the pile of clothes soon to come. Fire spread through my veins as Abbey's gaze traced each of my muscles, and she licked her lips. I'd never felt like this before, just from someone looking at me. Sitting forward, she ran a hand lightly along my abs. My muscles flexed under her touch, and her fingers tracing my skin left a heated trail in their wake.

Liam stepped up next to me, shirtless. Abbey switched her attention to him, and I took in how she marveled at his physique as well. Her hand landed on his abdomen, and she raked her nails lightly over the muscles. Liam sucked in a breath and flexed his muscles against her touch. We were different in build but equally in shape. We both had to stay in peak physical form to do our jobs.

Abbey's fingers reached Liam's belt buckle, and she looked at each of us in turn. I nodded, and the clicking of the buckle echoed around the room. My cock strained against my zipper, and I didn't know how much longer I could keep it contained. She made quick work of Liam's pants, letting them hit the floor along with his briefs, and then turned her focus on me. I had to hold my breath to stop myself from coming. Football stats scrambled through my brain, but they only reminded me of Abbey's love for the game.

My cock jutted straight at her when it was freed from my briefs. Abbey appraised both of us, standing in front of her in all our naked glory. Her eyes landed on my cock, and I could feel it grow impossibly hard. I had never been so thankful for all the work I put into staying in shape. I wanted Abbey to look at me every day with the same hunger she had at this very moment.

"Do you like what you see, darlin'?"

She lightly ran her fingers along the underside of our cocks. We let out simultaneous hisses.

"I need to be inside you, or I'm going to come if you keep touching me." I rocked back on my heels, needing to get away from her touch but also not wanting her to stop.

"Isn't that the point?" She looked up through her dark lashes and bit her lip.

Fuck.

Me.

Sideways.

"You can touch me all you want, darlin', after I get to come inside you and feel your pussy milk me for all it's worth."

Liam stepped out of her grasp and hurried to the bedside table.

Her mouth hung open. I could see the need in her eyes as they clouded over with desire. It mirrored mine. She needed my cock as much as I needed her. Needed to dive between those creamy legs and feel her wrap them around me as I claimed her.

Liam tossed me a condom from the drawer, and I made quick work of it. Abbey scrambled farther up the bed and sent me a welcoming smile, as though wondering why I was taking so long.

I eagerly climbed after her, crawling over her body until I could stare into her eyes. We gazed at each other, not needing words to communicate our desire. I brushed a piece of hair that had fallen across her forehead behind her ear and trailed my fingertips down the side of her neck. She sucked in a quick breath and shifted restlessly beneath me.

She opened her legs to let me further settle between them. My cock nestled against her heated core, and I rocked against her perfect body. I wanted her to enjoy every second of our time together. For her to know how special she was. How much I needed her.

I slid a finger between her pussy lips. She was still dripping wet, her arousal coating her inner thighs. I grabbed my cock and ran the tip through her wetness. Her moan and press of her hips against mine had me wanting to speed this up, but I continued to tease her. Easing my dick up and down her lips, coating the condom in her essence, was just as much for her as it was for me.

When I notched at her entrance, she locked eyes with me and nodded. I eased in slowly, not wanting to hurt her with my size. Abbey gasped beneath me, her hips shifting as I slipped in an inch, retreated, and then pushed in a little farther. When I was fully seated, my balls resting against her ass, I moaned deep.

"So tight. So hot. So fucking good." She was everything I never knew I needed.

Abbey wrapped her legs around my hips and wiggled beneath me.

I wanted to give her time to adjust, but she had other plans. I groaned, forcing myself to stay still. "You okay, darlin'?"

"Yes. Oh God. So full." Abbey's head tilted, exposing

her long neck. I nipped at the soft skin. She whimpered and grew wetter. I groaned, then pulled almost all the way out before sliding back in. She felt so damn good.

"If you don't start fucking me faster and harder right now, I'm going to go insane." Abbey wrapped her hands around my biceps. The bite of her nails dug into my skin, showing me how much she meant her words. I let out a snarl, pulled out to the tip, and slammed in all the way. Her cries of pleasure were music to my ears.

The bed dipped as Liam joined us. I lifted off the bed and settled her on my knees, keeping us entwined and connected. If she wanted me to fuck her, I was going to give her what she needed.

I thrust in and out slowly at first, letting her get used to this new angle, then picked up speed until her tits bounced with every thrust. I was almost disappointed when Liam grabbed her breasts and started playing with them. But when he tweaked her nipples and her pussy clenched down on my cock, I no longer had any envy.

Abbey turned her head and stared at Liam's cock. When she licked her lips, I knew she needed to give him the attention he deserved. I pulled out, ignoring her protests, and scooted out of the way. "Turn over, darlin.'"

She immediately scrambled to her hands and knees, thrusting her ass in my direction.

"Now, take Liam's cock in your mouth and suck him off while I fuck you."

She nodded and wrapped her hand around Liam's girth. I watched as her tongue licked the tip of his cock, swiping away the drop of pre-cum that had beaded. His moans increased when she sucked the head into her mouth.

I lined myself up with her opening and gave one hard thrust, burying myself to the hilt. Abbey moaned around Liam's cock with each rock of my hips. Liam gripped Abbey's shoulder to steady her while I continued to pound her deliciously hot pussy.

The tingling started in the base of my spine, and I knew I was going to come soon, but I needed to take care of Abbey first. Reaching around, I found her clit and circled it. Abbey moaned and rocked her hips, meeting mine with every thrust.

"Your mouth feels so good, *dulcinée*. Do you want me to come down that pretty throat of yours?"

Abbey nodded as she bobbed her head on Liam's cock, unable to speak with her mouth so full.

I increased the pressure and speed on her clit, feeling her walls clench around me. She was close to coming. When I pinched the little nub, her pussy fluttered and pulsed as her orgasm washed over her. Her muffled scream was like a trigger, and Liam muttered words in French as he came. She sucked him dry and licked along his length before he collapsed on the bed. My body tightened as my release washed over me. I came as her pussy continued to milk everything from me.

Our heavy breathing was a symphony in the quiet room. When Abbey caught her breath, I gently pulled out and let her collapse on the bed next to Liam. A pretty pink flush washed over her face and body. Her eyes had fluttered closed, and she relaxed onto the bed next to Liam, who was gently running his fingertips along her upper back and shoulders. I didn't want to leave her side, but I needed to clean up and make sure she was well taken care of.

When I returned from the bathroom with a damp towel, Liam offered to take it from me, but deep down, I knew I wouldn't be satisfied unless I did it. She gasped as I ran the cloth along her pussy, no doubt sore from so much attention.

I tossed the cloth to the floor and climbed onto the bed to join them. The need to hold Abbey close was overwhelming. I didn't know why, but I knew if I didn't, I wouldn't be able to rest. It seemed we all needed a good nap. Abbey had flipped over to her back, and I rested my hand on her hip while Liam continued to stroke her arm, leaving goosebumps in his wake.

She was perfect for us. I still didn't want her to see how broken I was, but in this moment, I didn't care about a thing except for making sure I did everything to keep Abbey right there with us.

"Is that what sex is supposed to be like?" Her soft voice filtered through my thoughts.

"Yes," I answered softly, realizing this was important.

"Maybe a little extra, since there are two of us. Why?" Liam and I stared at her. She'd mentioned earlier she hadn't orgasmed in years. Now I wondered how long her ex had ignored her needs.

"Because it's *never* been like that for me." A dreamy smile tugged at her lips as she closed her eyes and drifted off to sleep.

I looked at Liam, and he shrugged. I wanted to admit

it'd never been like this for me either, but her breathing had evened out, and I didn't want to chance waking her.

With Abbey in the middle, Liam and I shifted to settle in around her. I wrapped my arm around her middle and pulled her close, settling her against my chest. Abbey slung her arm around Liam's waist, and he moved in beside her.

It didn't take long for me to drift to sleep, waking an hour later to Abbey moaning. She was turned toward me, with Liam buried deep inside her from behind. This time I got to see her face as she reached her climax—the way her eyes fluttered shut and mouth opened in a silent scream. It made me rock hard in an instant and wanting to dive between her legs the moment Liam pulled out, but she needed time.

"Hungry, darlin'?" I asked when her stomach growled an hour later. We had just finished fucking again and were laying lazily in bed, waiting for us all to catch our breaths.

"Ravenous," she said, licking her lips. I groaned, thinking about how that tongue had licked every inch of my dick earlier.

"What do we even have in the kitchen?" Liam kissed Abbey's bare shoulder.

"Stay right there, darlin'. Liam and I will find something to eat for us," I said, tapping Abbey on the nose and venturing to the kitchen.

We put together a buffet of all the things we had left to eat in the house for dinner and fed it to Abbey in bed. Then we had Abbey again for dessert. It was one of the best days off I'd had in forever. I didn't want to think about going to work the next day. It was going to be tough to leave Abbey for my night shift. I'd only had her for eight hours, and I was addicted to her already.

The sun peeking through the windows was my only indication of the time. I'd missed waking up for my run but wasn't disappointed about it. I felt refreshed and had the best sleep I'd had in a long time. It wasn't until the chime of a missed call and then an incoming call had me realizing what woke me in the first place.

My phone rang again from my discarded pants somewhere on the floor. Unwrapping myself from Abbey's warm body, I found the culprit and saw it was Gavin. As much as I didn't want to answer, I had to. What if Blake was going into labor or there was an emergency on the ranch?

"What's wrong, Gav?" I whispered, not wanting to wake anyone.

"You know I wouldn't call you unless it was an emergency." His voice sounded strained. I didn't like it.

"I know. What's going on? Is Blake okay?"

"She's good. It's about the ranch. We had a breach in the fence, on the back lot by the road. We aren't sure how many heads got out yet."

"I'm on my way. Let's round up some guys and see if we can't get the escapees." I glanced over at Abbey. So much for spending the day with her. This took precedence and not knowing how much cattle we lost, it could take all day to rustle them up.

"Duke, it's not just that." I tensed, waiting for his next words. "The wire looks like it was cut." *Fuck.*

"Who would come this far out here to vandalize our ranch?"

"I have no idea. You need to come take a look."

"Let me grab Maverick, and I'll call you for your location."

I disconnected and caught Liam's eyes in the dim light. He gave a firm nod, and I knew he'd heard everything. As much as I didn't want to leave Abbey after the night we'd had, I had work to do. I had a ranch to keep safe, which also meant keeping her safe.

ABBEY

$\mathcal{W}$hen I woke, I was sprawled across Liam. Duke was gone. When I asked Liam where he went off to so early, he said Duke had some business to take care of. My stomach twisted, thinking maybe yesterday was too much, and he was avoiding me. The past few days, I'd discovered Duke had a routine. He got up early, went for a run, and then came home, showered, and made breakfast. Duke was nowhere to be found, the kitchen was empty, and Jax was asleep on the couch.

What if he didn't enjoy last night as much as I had? Maybe it was only supposed to be one night, and today we were going back to the way things were. My heart ached at that thought. I'd had the best sex of my life with Duke and Liam, and I didn't want to go back. I wanted more of it. It sure felt like Liam wanted that too, by the way he kissed me before I left to meet the girls. It had taken a lot of convincing to let me go to breakfast without him. If he had his way, he would be feeding me breakfast in bed.

As much as I didn't want to think it, we needed to get back to the reality of things. I lived in another state, and I just came out of a terrible relationship. I knew I needed to get home and pack my things. I needed to find a new place to live and a job.

I took my notebook with me, so I could start making a list of the things I needed to get done. "Do any of you know of any job openings around here?" I asked between bites of my pancakes.

"Why do you need a job, Abbs?" Blake's eyebrows furrowed.

"I need to make some money." I sighed, wishing I'd never let Jeff convince me not to work. "I can't very well go back to Jeff's. And I don't have enough money saved for first *and* last month's rent on a new place."

"What about Liam and Duke?" Grace's lips turned down.

"What about them?" It was foolish of me to think I had forever with them after just one night.

"Don't you like them?" Grace's eyebrows knitted together, and her forehead scrunched. I knew it was going to be hard to leave my best friends, but my life wasn't here.

"Of course I do, but it's just some rebound fling. I'm only here until I can get my feet under me." I blew out a breath.

"There's no such thing as a fling around here. We all should know," Victoria said around her mouthful. It was her idea for pancakes this morning. It was her most recent pregnancy craving and we all happily indulged.

"Have you slept with them yet?" Jessie prodded.

My entire face heated. "Slept" felt like such an under-statement for what we did.

"Oh. My. God. You have," Grace squealed. "Please tell me those two are trying their damnedest to convince you to stay."

"Grace, it just happened. Will you please keep your voice down?" I looked around the empty dining hall. There was no one in here except for us and a few other staff members.

"Only if you tell me how it was." Grace waggled her eyebrows.

"It was amazing," I admitted, my breathy voice sounding foreign to my ears.

"I knew it," she squeaked. "Those two are an intense combo."

"Are you sure you're okay with it?" I asked. "I mean, you have known Liam for forever." I didn't want to put an awkward strain on any of our relationships if things really didn't work out with the guys. I'd also never considered if either Blake or Grace had any romantic feelings for Liam in the past.

"He's like a brother to me. I don't see where this is going." Her forehead creased, and I laughed.

"As long as those two are taking care of you, then we have no problem with you claiming them as yours." Blake patted my hand.

"Where is everyone this morning?" Alex walked in, looking around.

"There was a breach in one of the fences. Everyone went to go round up all the escapees." Jessie waved her over to join us.

So that must have been where Duke went off to. My chest tightened; I'd immediately thought the worst. This was what Jeff had done to me—always assuming the bad before the good. I hated it.

"But you are planning on staying around for a while longer? You have to stay for the baby shower, and I want you to be here when the baby comes." Blake picked up our conversation.

"I don't know. I hadn't really thought about much past getting away from Jeff. As much as I would love to stay, I don't want to be a burden." My fingers traced the veins in the wood of the table.

"Honey, you're welcome to stay as long as you want. I'm sure your men will be trying to convince you to stay forever as soon as you see them again." Jessie smiled.

I let out a deep sigh. If what we did yesterday was any part of this convincing, I was all for them convincing me some more.

"Oh, she's got it bad. Look at that smile on her face." Victoria pointed with her fork, and everyone started to laugh. I joined their laughter. She was right, of course.

"Well, that's settled. Abbey is staying for a little while longer. So, please tell me we're still on for shopping and partying this weekend?" Alex's pleading eyes landed on me. "You have to come with us."

All the girls answered their yeses.

"Absolutely," I said. Everyone here made me feel right at home. How could I pass up an opportunity to have a girl's day, especially when I hadn't had one in years? Besides Blake and Grace, I'd let all my other girlfriends go at Jeff's urging. I hadn't realized until now how isolating that had been.

"First things first. We need to go to town and do some shopping. I think Abbey could use a few more things if she's staying longer." Grace looked me up and down.

"Can we stop by the grocery store too? I want to pick up something for the house," I asked.

"You planning on cooking something for your men?" Jessie winked.

"I was just going to restock the fridge, but now I feel like I need to. Is there something I should know?"

"The quickest way to a man's heart is through his stomach," Jessie started, but all the girls finished.

I laughed. "I have a feeling there are lots of stories I need to hear about later. What should I cook? Something French?"

"Liam loves anything. And so does Duke." Jessie tapped her chin. "Do you know how to make a Bolognese sauce?"

"That's a type of meat sauce, right?" I'd heard of it but never made it before.

She nodded. "Exactly, just a fancier version."

"No, but I could look up recipes and try it." I had cooked a lot for me and Jeff and loved to try out new recipes.

"I'll give you a list of ingredients. Duke loves a good pasta dish." Jessie grabbed a pen and paper. She handed me the list when she finished, and I stuffed it in my pocket for later. Butterflies fluttered in my stomach. They'd treated me so well. I wanted to repay their kindness.

Once we'd finished, the sun had peeked from behind the morning clouds and was glowing. We could see a few of the ranch hands wandering around, but one in particular caught my eye.

Duke.

He came out of the barn with a few others as we were leaving the dining hall. He took his hat off his head and ran his hand over his short, dark hair and around the back of his neck. When he stepped into the sunlight, I could see his weary expression, and I had to wonder how serious this fence issue was.

"Speaking of your men, there's one right now." Alex nudged me, and I didn't fight the smile that stretched across my face. My heart beat against my chest, and I couldn't take my eyes off of him. He seemed stressed, and I wanted to go over and see if there was anything I could do to help, but I didn't know if that was something he'd *want* me to do.

Duke caught sight of our group, said something to the men, then jogged over. He looked so good in his jeans and shirt. Images of his naked body from last night made their way into my mind. In the short-sleeved shirt he was currently wearing, I could only see a portion of his tattoos. I knew they stretched all the way up his arm and around his chest and back.

"Morning, darlin'. I'm sorry I wasn't there when you woke up." His voice was low for only me to hear, but I had no doubt the girls were straining their ears. Again, he stood slightly to the side to block the sun from my face as I looked up at him.

"It's okay. Next time wake me so I have a chance to say

goodbye." I bit my lip, not believing I'd said that out loud. I cringed inside, wondering if he'd tell me there wasn't going to be another time.

The corner of his mouth lifted. "I'll make sure I do. There's some stuff I need to take care of around here, and then I have patrol. I'm hoping to see you before my shift, but if not, I'll see you in the morning."

"Okay. Be safe." I wanted to swoon on the spot. It was like he was a different person after yesterday—not totally grumpy but opening up just the littlest bit.

He nodded and started to leave, then turned back around. "I forgot something."

"What?"

"This," he said before catching my chin in his fingers and kissing me in front of everyone. It wasn't just a chaste kiss either. It was full of promises of what he would rather do. He nipped at my bottom lip before pulling away.

I sighed, watching his retreating form. Now I *really* wanted to stay here forever. In the last few days, Liam and Duke had shown me more compassion and kindness than Jeff had in all the years I was with him.

I was still watching Duke when the girls crowded around me.

"That was hot." Jessie fanned herself.

"Look at that. Mr. Grump has a heart." Grace laughed.

"I think you mean Officer Sexypants," Victoria joked.

I felt the flood of embarrassment, but I knew it was for nothing. I'd have him do that again every day. It's not as if the girls minded.

"Okay. Okay. Let's get ready and go to town," I said,

walking away. When I walked into the house, Liam was in the kitchen, putting away dishes.

"Did you have a good breakfast with the girls?" he asked.

"I did. We're going to go to town to do some shopping. Anything I can pick up while I'm there?" I leaned against the counter and watched him move so fluidly around the kitchen.

"Nothing I can think of right now. Just be careful." He stopped and pressed a kiss to my forehead. I sighed. I think forehead kisses were my new favorite thing.

"I'm going to go grab my bag and head out." I went to my room and got my things together before I decided to stay behind with him all day.

"Have a good day, Liam. I'll see you tonight." I waved at him as I passed the kitchen on the way out.

"*Dulcinée.*" Liam's voice was deeper than I'd ever heard it. I froze in place. Had I made him mad? I swallowed and forced myself to face him.

"Yes?" I couldn't hide the quiver in my voice and winced.

He met me in the hallway. He must have noticed my reaction because his eyes softened as he wrapped his hand around the back of my neck. "Hey," he whispered. "You okay?"

I took a deep breath and nodded. He wasn't mad at me. Duke and Liam were nothing like Jeff. I needed to remember that. When his lips landed on mine, the tension fell away.

Liam hummed against my lips before reluctantly stepping back. "Have fun. Be safe."

"I will." He walked me to the door. "I didn't ask you what you were going to do today."

"Taking Zeus out for a ride. He needs a good workout now that he's been cleared by Caleb." He gave me another quick kiss.

"Then I guess I should be telling you to be safe too." I snuggled in his embrace, enjoying the flutters in my body at being near him.

"Go before I cancel all our plans for the day and take you to bed," he growled in my ear then swatted my ass as he sent me out the door.

I giggled but didn't stop. Glancing over my shoulder, I could see Liam and Jax standing in the doorway, watching me leave. My heart soared. After yesterday, I wasn't certain how everything would play out, but it looked like I was worried about nothing.

"Come on, girl. Let's go, let's go," Grace called from the ranch's SUV. "Took you long enough."

I piled in the backseat along with Alex and Jessie. As we headed to town, the girls chatted about wedding details, and my mind wandered to last night. They'd both been very thorough in making sure I was well satisfied. My face heated as I remembered just how satisfied I'd been.

I couldn't believe the drastic differences in them. Duke with his body, hot as sin. It should be illegal to look that good. The scars and tattoos made him look even more delicious. His grumpiness was only a mask for everyone else. He showed me his true self, and it was intense. He made me feel desired and safe—things I'd never felt before I met him.

And Liam with his lean, muscular frame that looked sculpted from stone. The splatter of hair across his chest and the trail that lead from his navel to his impressive member... I had to wonder if Liam would let me explore his body more tonight, or if he had other plans. When we were together, he had a dominance that gave me the courage to explore things I'd never done before. He was caring and gentle, and he had this need to always be near me.

The more I thought about Duke and Liam, the more I realized how much I liked them, and how much I missed them when they weren't around. My heart thudded in my chest. I was falling for them. How could I fall after a few days? What could this possibly mean and how could I be sure my heart wouldn't be shattered when I eventually left?

LIAM

I walked into the second barn to look for Duke. When I messaged him to find out information, he let me know he needed to grab supplies before heading to the broken fence. He was very short in his messages, and it had me worried, considering what I'd overheard from his conversation this morning.

A group was gathered near the supply room. Their words were low and hard to hear over the sounds of the nickers and snorts from the remaining horses. I didn't try to hide my steps as I approached them. I picked up a few words like *cut*, *vandalism*, and *sabotage* as I got closer.

"Let's not tell the girls yet. It could have been some teenagers looking for fun," Declan said once I'd joined the group. Declan and Thomas, the ranch owners, were huddled with Duke, Matt, one of the stable hands, and Gavin.

"I agree," Duke said. Since he'd woken this morning, the usual serious Duke was firmly in place.

"Have you checked the cameras to see if they caught anything?" Thomas asked Duke.

"They're being downloaded as we speak, and I'll watch them tonight." He sighed. With Duke's training, I could already guess he had a list of other things he wanted to do in his head.

Duke was clearly going to be very busy over the next few days between handling this and his shifts. My stomach twisted. I'd already seen the positive changes in Duke since Abbey came into our lives. What if he reverted to how closed off he was before or convinced himself not to pursue her? Knowing Duke, he'd tell himself he couldn't be with Abbey for a variety of reasons.

And what about Abbey? Clearly, the man in her last relationship didn't take care of her needs. What if she thought Duke didn't want her because he had to give his attention to the vandalism? He and I were both in this. I had to make sure we nurtured what we'd started. I knew Abbey was the one for us.

I hadn't spoken with him since we'd had our first taste of her. I'd spent the last eight years trying to get Duke to loosen up and come back to life after his deployment and academy training. Last night, I saw a side of him I'd never seen before—one I wanted to see more of. He didn't close himself off like he usually did, and he doted on Abbey like she was already his. Plus, he didn't have a nightmare last night. And Abbey was the one to get him to that contentment.

As much as I was worried about him not being able to

find time for her right now, I was sure he'd find little ways to show her he was there for her. At least I hoped so.

"I heard about what happened. What do you need me to do?" I looked around at each of the men in the circle. "The girls left for town to go shopping."

Thomas' shoulders dropped as he let out a breath. "Good. Has anyone heard from Travis or Ryder?" Of course they already had their cattle teams out and about, checking the rest of the property.

"Ryder checked in and said his group found about ten heads." Gavin pulled out his phone. "Travis hasn't checked in yet."

"Ty and Scott were doing a head count. I don't know how long that will take." Gavin unclipped his satellite phone from his belt and dialed. He stepped aside to speak with whoever he just called, but we all stayed quiet to listen for an update.

"You're guessing around forty?" Gavin cursed under his breath while he listened to more updates. "Okay, keep looking. I'll let the scouts know and have them keep searching. We've found at least ten so far."

Shit. Forty heads lost. That was not good.

Just then, Gavin's cell rang, and Duke grabbed it from his belt clip to answer it. "Travis? Please have good news." Duke's face snapped up with whatever the reply was. "Okay. I'm on my way."

He handed the cell to Gavin, and his jaw ticked.

"What did Travis say?" We were all on edge. Nothing like this had ever happened at King's Ranch. This why we had rotations to look out for the cattle and patrols riding the fences.

"Another mile down from the first breach is another. Plus, two downed heifers. Andrew is leaving his group now to ride to Travis." Being one of King's Ranch's resident vets, Andrew would need to investigate the cause of death for the two heifers.

"Fuck," Declan yelled and kicked the nearest trunk in the aisle. The longhorns were his babies. "We need to get out there now, Duke."

"Did they say anything else?" Matt asked. I had to wonder why he'd stayed behind, but if everyone was out, then someone was needed with Gavin.

"No." Duke turned to me. "I'm going to grab the SUV and head there with Dec. Can you take care of Mav?"

He'd taken his horse, Maverick, to check the fence this morning. I had no issue taking care of him so Duke could get out there quicker. I set a hand on his shoulder. "Go. I've got it covered here."

"Do what you can to make sure the girls are none the wiser. At least until we have more details."

I gave a firm nod. I hadn't seen Victoria in the car with them, but I'd find out who was left and find some way to distract them.

I had no doubt in the next few days, the team would make sure the winter pastures were secure and start the winter drive sooner than planned. It wasn't ideal, but with something like this happening, it was the best thing we could do. We couldn't afford to lose any more cattle before the auction.

When I finished tucking Maverick into his stall, I made my way to the office in search of Gavin. I figured an extra pair of hands was an extra pair of hands. Whether I knew anything about cattle or fixing fences, I'd find some way to help. That's how we did things at King's Ranch. Everyone did what they could to lighten the load.

"Hey, Liam. Do you need something?" Gavin glanced up from his computer where Matt was pointing at the screen when I knocked.

I leaned against the doorframe and crossed my arms over my chest. "Just wondering what I can do to help. I know everyone else is out running around, but do you have anything here that needs some attention?"

"I can't think of anything at the moment. Except the girls. Have you heard from them yet?"

"No, but I can reach out to them. They should be in town by now. I'll see who went with them and what time they think they might be back."

Wandering around the barn, I opened my text thread to Blake and thought about how I should start. I didn't want to sound nosy, and I didn't want to alert the girls that something was wrong. Otherwise, they might cut their trip short, and I wanted Abbey to have time to bond with them. The happier she was, the more likely we could convince her to stay.

The first stop was likely shopping, and I wanted to make sure Abbey got what she needed. I remembered looking through her sketchbook and noticing she only had a few blank pages left. Maybe Blake could help me look for something she liked while they were in town.

I didn't bother opening with a greeting. We'd never made a point of doing that in the first place. Why start now?

Liam: See if you can find any sketchbooks while in town. If you can, will you grab one for me, please? Abbey needs another one.

Blake: Why don't you tell her to get another one yourself?

Liam: Just do it for me. And be discreet. I want this to be a surprise. And if she needs anything else, let me know, and I'll pay for it.

Blake: Okay, fine. Only because sweet things like this will help Abbs decide to stay here longer.

Liam: She wants to leave?

My heart thudded in my chest.

Blake: You need to sit down and talk with her. And do a whole lot of convincing.

Liam: On it, boss.

I let a few seconds pass before I did my recon.

Liam: Who went with you?

Blake: Abbey, Grace, Jessie, and Alex. Why?

Liam: Just wondering who was left here. It's like a ghost town.

I hoped that would keep her from asking too many questions.

> Blake: Tori had work to do and stayed behind. She should be in her office. I didn't have anyone scheduled for training today, so I think most of the other riders are enjoying a day off. Maybe you should too.

> Liam: You're funny. Zeus needs his butt back in shape for the season.

> Blake: Okay. I'll call you later, and we can schedule a session.

> Liam: Sounds good. Go enjoy the day. And lunch is on me. Have fun.

I found myself already walking to Gavin's office before I'd finished texting Blake.

"All clear with the girls in town. Only one who didn't go was Victoria. I'm going to see if I can distract her." I thumbed over my shoulder toward the big house.

Gavin laughed. "Good luck with that."

Victoria was right where she was supposed to be—glued to her desk. I knocked lightly on the door and smiled when she looked up. It didn't surprise me she hadn't gone with the girls. Her pregnancy was a little rougher than Blake's, considering she was carrying twins.

"Hey, Liam." Her smile stretched across her face. I was glad she had found love with the twins, Caleb and Andrew, after everything she'd been through. I'd known her just as long as I'd known the Kingstons, and she'd had it pretty rough—going from one arranged marriage to the next and no one ever taking her seriously. She fit in perfectly on the ranch and made a great addition to the team. She was the one who had organized the event last week in New York.

"Hey, Tori. Do you have a minute?"

"Sure. Sit down." She gestured to the chairs in front of her desk. I took a seat and collected my thoughts.

"I wanted to ask for some advice. It's about Abbey."

I didn't think her smile could have grown any bigger, but it did. She rubbed her hands together. "I don't know her the best, but I can try."

"Duke and I think she's the one. We just don't know how to tell her or how to ask her to stay." Duke and I hadn't talked about what last night meant, but I knew he felt the same as I did. When the other guys described just knowing, I'd scoffed at it, but now that Abbey was here, I understood.

"I wanted to do something special for her, to show her we want her to stay with us." I rubbed at the back of my neck. "But I don't want to scare her off."

"What have you done so far?"

"Not much, really. We've hung out a few times, and last night was the first night we were all together." Heat filled my cheeks.

"Well, that changes things a little." She tapped a finger to her chin.

"I know she loves to draw. I've asked Blake to find a sketchbook while they're in town." I knew that wasn't going to be enough, but I was out of ideas. It also made me want to get to know everything about Abbey, so I could anticipate her needs and her wants.

"She also loves to paint but hasn't been able to in a long time. She mentioned she loved going to the parks to paint, but she had to stop after a while. Maybe I can surprise her with an outing and new paints to use."

"That's a great idea. Why did she stop?" I sat up straight. There was clearly more to the story than Tori was saying.

"You'll have to ask her." She shrugged, letting me know without words there was something she couldn't say.

"There aren't any art supply stores in town. Do you think you can help me order some? I don't know anything about paints or what she might need. I've seen her draw-ings of the horses and the ranch so far. She's amazing. I want to do everything in my power for her to be able to see herself living here with us."

"I'm glad you said that. She was talking about needing to find a job to save money for when she went back home. Maybe you need to reassure her that her place is here."

My heart leapt in my throat. Tori was the second person to mention that Abbey wanted to leave. I needed to make sure she knew how much we wanted her to stay. She needed to know she was ours. We needed a plan.

After Tori helped order various art supplies she'd heard Abbey mention and had them express shipped, I gave Zeus a lighter workout than I'd intended before heading to the house with Jax. I knew Duke needed to come home before work, and I wanted to hash out a few things with him before he left for the evening.

When I entered the kitchen, Duke was already prepping coffee to take to work with him.

"Hey, *mon pote.* Any updates?"

He smiled at my familiar greeting of *my friend.* "All the remaining heads have been rounded up. Both spots where the fence is down look like they were cut. Unfortunately, Andrew doesn't have a cause of death for the two heifers, but my gut tells me it was foul play. Something is up, and I don't like it." His jaw ticked as he paced the kitchen. "The files are downloading from the trail cameras. I'll look them over tonight when I have down time."

"Do you want me to make a fresh pot before bed, so you can make a stop in during the night?" I asked.

"No, it's fine. It'll be too tempting to stay if I come back." He shrugged.

I wasn't fooled by his easy-going attitude. With a smile, I leaned against the counter. "Glad you mentioned that. We need to talk about Abbey."

He stared at me, his throat bobbing as he swallowed hard.

I pushed on, pretty sure he was on the same page as me but needing to know for sure. "I think she's the one for us. Not think... I *know* she is." I thumped my fingers on the counter.

He nodded. "I've been feeling it too. I just don't want to scare her away with all my problems."

"You haven't yet. She even slept with you through an episode."

"She helped me through one in town too." Since he'd shaved for work tonight, I could see the hint of color grace his cheeks. He hated to admit he had any weaknesses.

"You didn't tell me about that. What happened?"

He ran a hand down his face. "I don't want to go into details, but she pulled me out. She does something to me I can't deny. I want her to stay."

"So do I. What do we need to do for her to figure out the same thing?"

"I don't know. I was hoping you'd come up with something. You know I'm not great at that stuff."

I chuckled. He wasn't wrong. Out of the two of us, I was more in touch with my feelings. "True."

We stood there, staring off into space for a few moments. "From the little she's said and from something Tori mentioned earlier, I don't think she had a supportive relationship with her ex. I want to show her we're different, that her wishes and needs are important to us."

He nodded.

"I talked to Tori earlier. She mentioned Abbey liked to paint. I ordered supplies for her. Maybe we can take her to a park or somewhere special to paint."

"That's good." Duke poured the coffee into his travel mug. "What else?"

"She needs to know we're serious. This isn't just a fling, but I don't want to scare her off too soon. I figured maybe if we can convince her to sleep in bed with us from now on, then we could sort of turn her room into a studio. She could paint and draw to her heart's content."

"And what would you like to see me draw or paint?"

Duke and I nearly jumped out of our skins. It was rare

for anyone to surprise him. He always heard them from a mile away.

Abbey stood in the doorway to the kitchen. My face was on fire, knowing she had caught us talking about her. Her smile was the only thing that eased my worries.

I cleared my throat. "How was your trip into town?" I asked, rubbing the back of my neck.

She let out a cute snort-laugh. "It was fun. I bought some clothes. But I'm more interested in hearing about what you're planning. Seems like you boys have been busy while I was gone." Her arms crossed over her chest. Her smile only grew wider at our grimaces.

What had she heard?

ABBEY

couldn't keep the smile off my face. I'd walked in and overheard Duke and Liam talking. It wasn't like I tried to be quiet coming in. Jax even greeted me at the door.

My heart soared when they mentioned they wanted me to stay. I wanted to laugh and cry with joy when Liam mentioned he'd already been working on a plan to win me over.

When Liam mentioned painting, I couldn't stay quiet any longer. I couldn't wait to get my hands dirty again. It'd been so long since I was able to paint. Jeff hated it. He was afraid I'd get paint all over the apartment and said it was pointless for me to waste money on paints and canvases when I wasn't going to do anything with them.

Duke and Liam *wanted* me to paint, to see the ranch and horses on canvas. Count me in.

"How much did you hear?" Duke's body tensed. His growl was less intimidating now that I knew how he felt. I smiled and placed my hand on his face.

"Enough." I stroked his cheek, and he leaned into my palm. "You shaved."

He didn't say anything, and I was pretty sure he was going to wait me out until I admitted what I'd heard. "I walked in when you were talking about when we were in town."

His shoulders drooped. "I have to get to work."

He was pulling in on himself, and I realized when he had an episode, he didn't want to expose me to his thoughts. He was afraid of scaring me off. "Hey, I'm happy I was able to be there for you. Okay?"

He grunted an acknowledgment.

At least it was a start. "Why this?" I patted his cheek and smiled. I thought he was ridiculously handsome either way, but I'd gotten used to the beard.

"Need to be clean shaven for work," he responded, his voice gruff.

"That's a shame. I like the scruff." I came up on my toes, and Duke met me halfway. Our lips touched, and I felt the hum of electricity run through my veins. Liam was behind me in a second, kissing my neck and stroking my sides.

I loved how they showed their affection. Fingers on my chin pulled me from Duke's lips, and Liam placed his upon mine.

"Can this be a regular thing?" I asked when he lifted his head from mine. I wanted to be greeted with their delicious kisses every time I saw them.

"What?" Duke kissed my shoulder.

"These kisses." I rubbed noses with Liam.

"I promise to kiss you every chance I get. Every time I see you." Liam let his lips brush over mine.

"Every opportunity I can, I would love to have my lips on you," Duke whispered in my ear, and my knees went weak. I could get used to this.

Duke placed me on the island. I loved the way his large body fit between my thighs. Liam stood next to him.

I looped one arm around Liam and the other around Duke. "So, you want me to stay here with you?"

"Yes," they said in unison.

"Are you sure?" I bit my lip. I didn't really want to leave and couldn't think of a reason why I had to. These two men made me feel like the person I was before things went bad with Jeff. I'd thought it was too soon to find love right after my breakup, but I felt more loved by them than I ever had with Jeff.

I was ready to knock down the wall I'd built around my heart. Their words and actions had started to heal all the hurt and suffering I'd faced. When the time was right, I wanted to share that with them, so they knew how much I appreciated the ways they made me happy.

There was a very good chance I was falling in love with them.

"*Dulcinée*, we don't want you to leave. We think you belong here with us." Liam rubbed his palm against my waist.

I sucked in a breath. It was one thing to overhear them say these things about me. It was another to have them tell me to my face. But I had to keep a level head. I needed to know exactly what they meant.

"Just for now? Or for more than that?"

Duke's hand slid up my thigh and squeezed. "Darlin', you have no clue what you've done to us."

"But we only met a few days ago, and we just slept together yesterday." As much as I wanted this, how could we all be so sure? What if they didn't want me in a week or two? What if they got tired of me?

"We want you for as long as you'll have us. We're hoping forever is on the table. We plan on sleeping with you every day from now on." Liam smiled.

"I've wanted you since you rolled down the window and flashed those pretty eyes at me." Duke lifted my hand and placed a kiss on my inner wrist. "Please say you'll stay."

He winced when his phone beeped. Glancing at the clock on the stove, I saw it was later than I'd thought. He was going to have to leave for work soon.

"We can talk about this later. It'll give you some time to think about it." Duke pulled back, but I grabbed his arm before he could move away.

I didn't want to have this conversation later. I wanted them to know what I wanted now. "Yes."

"*Pardon?*" Liam leaned closer.

"Yes, I'll stay with you. I want to be with you. Both of you."

Duke surged forward and landed a bruising kiss on my lips. I smiled into his kiss, laughing.

"Now I really don't want to go to work," he growled, stepping away to allow Liam to give me his own enthusiastic kiss. Life couldn't get any better than this. I was on top of the world with the two of them and the future I saw before us.

"What are your shifts like?" I asked Duke as he finished making his coffee in his travel mug.

"I only work part time, so it depends on the week. My schedule is three days on, four days off. Each week is different depending on what days my shifts fall on. I work ten-hour days and pick up an extra shift if needed. Tonight, I picked up a graveyard for one of the other guys who had a previous obligation. Otherwise, I would have been done with work today." He grumbled the last bit, making me smile. I didn't want him to go to work either. Now that we'd had a talk and I knew where I stood with them, it would have been nice to celebrate together. But I also understood he had a commitment to the town and his job.

"You come home when?" I tried to calculate it in my head, but I didn't know when his shift actually started.

"As soon as humanly possible, darlin'." He gave me a peck on the cheek but answered when I gave him a fake scowl. "I should be home before you wake up. Especially if Liam does a good job of tiring you out tonight."

"You won't be jealous I'm with Liam alone?" I cocked my head. If we were going to make the three of us work, I needed to know how they felt about time I spent with each of them.

"Yes... and no. Of course I'm going to be jealous he has you all to himself, but there will be times when he's at a horse show and I get my turn. But knowing he is taking care of you is enough to get me through my shift." He brushed a thumb along my cheekbone. My chest tightened at his tender caress. I loved seeing his grumpiness slip away and his sweet side shine through.

"Okay. I just wanted to make sure you were okay with it." I grabbed the front of his uniform and pulled him in between my legs. "Just make sure you're home before I wake up." I wanted to give him a proper goodbye kiss filled with promise before he left again.

My tongue dueled with his, and by the time I let him go, we were both panting. "Enjoy your night, darlin'. Think of me." His lips turned up against mine.

"I'll try. I'll miss you" He nipped at my lips one more time before reluctantly pulling away and heading out the front door.

Liam wiped down the kitchen island. "What would you like to do tonight?"

I jumped off the counter. "Oh my gosh, I almost forgot. Would you mind helping me unload everything I bought today?"

Liam's eyebrows knitted together. "Unload? Woman, what did you buy?"

I chuckled and walked out to Blake's SUV without a word. I popped the hatchback to reveal my bags. A few were full of clothes and others were filled with groceries.

"I was planning on making dinner one of these nights, so I got what I needed in town while I was there." I took one of the bags with my clothes, and before I could grab another, Liam had both his arms loaded with the rest. "You know I can take some of those." I smiled at him. He really was so sweet.

"One is enough," he said as I hit the automatic close button for the hatch.

"Let's get this stuff put away and find something for dinner." Liam kept pace with me, even though I knew his long legs could eat up the distance to the house in half the time.

"What dish did you have in mind to make this week?" he asked as we put away the groceries.

"It was supposed to be a surprise, but I'm never good with those." I shrugged. "I was going to make a pasta Bolognese with a fresh salad and cheesecake for dessert."

"That sounds divine. We can do that in a couple of days so Duke can have it when he gets home. With work tonight, his shifts this stretch are all messed up."

"Works for me. What do you want to do tonight?" I laughed at Liam's waggling eyebrows. "I meant for dinner."

"I could eat you for dinner *and* dessert," he growled, kissing my neck.

I gave him a little shove, and Liam stepped back, grabbing my waist, and directed me toward the counter. Caging me in, his warm body pressed against mine, and a fire lit between my thighs.

I needed him.

Duke and Liam had woken something inside of me.

I wanted Liam. I wanted to ride him. I'd never done that before, but I had a feeling he wouldn't object.

Liam leaned down so we were eye level. "Let's grab some dinner at the dining hall, and then you are all mine."

I felt my cheeks heat. "Okay." If only he knew what I had in mind for tonight. We went, and it seemed like the quickest dinner of my life. It felt like there was no one else in that hall with us as we ate. We couldn't keep our eyes off each other. Liam sat next to me, leaving little space between us. He scarfed his dinner with his hand firmly in place on my thigh. His fingers stroked along my jeans, inching higher and higher until I had to squeeze my legs shut to stop him. His chuckle told me he knew exactly what he was doing to me—pure torture.

On the way to the house, we weren't fast enough for Liam's liking. He tossed me over his shoulder. Not that I minded. His toned backside was my view the entire way. He didn't stop until we were in his room and he flipped me onto the bed.

I scrambled to sit up, and Liam's hands were on me quicker than I could get to him. Articles of clothing were tossed around the room as we stripped each other in a hurry.

"Is this how it's going to be every night?" I murmured. I'd never felt like this before—the uncontrollable need to touch someone, to feel their touch on me.

"Every night you're with us." Liam licked his lips.

My eyes traced the small movement, wishing it was my tongue. I threaded my fingers in his hair and pulled him to me. His arms went around my waist until his hands cupped my ass. I moaned as his skin met mine. This is what I'd been craving. He tucked me in closer against his solid frame.

Our mouths fused together as we rocked and touched each other. His kiss heightened my arousal. Between having his cock against my pussy, the tension from dinner, and the way he used his tongue, I was already close to coming.

Liam slipped his hand between us. When his fingers found my clit, swollen and ready for him, he only had to circle twice, and I was crying out my pleasure. He dipped lower as he traced my slit and pumped his fingers into me. The sounds my body made with each time surge reminded me how wet I was for him. It only took a few seconds more before my body tightened and pulsed around his digits.

"Beautiful," Liam said. "You are so responsive; it's just beautiful."

I wrapped my hand around his hard length. He moaned, and his hips gave a tiny thrust into my palm. I slowly stroked him, but he pushed my hand away before I could work him the way I wanted to.

I pouted, and he nipped my protruding lip. "If you keep touching me, I'm going to come, and we can't have that. Not yet, at least." He winked as he gave my chest a tiny push, and I collapsed on the bed. Liam put one hand on each of my knees and opened my legs.

"Look at how wet you are. Have you been like this all night?"

I nodded, sucking my bottom lip between my teeth.

"One orgasm wasn't enough. You need a few more before the night is over."

I whimpered at Liam's words. Then he kissed his way from my navel to my apex, then down my thighs and back up. I was wiggling with need by the time he made it to my clit. I knew as soon as he put his mouth on me, I was going to come just as quickly as before.

Liam's hot breath fanned my lower lips, and his tongue swiped out, taking one long lick from my opening to my swollen nub. *Fuck*. I felt like I was ready to explode.

I lifted my hips, restlessly feeding my pussy to him. When he slid two fingers inside me, my imagination went wild. I could feel every inch, and I wanted to feel his cock just the same. He pumped his fingers and sucked hard on my clit, my orgasm slamming into me.

"I'm coming." My hips bucked against his mouth.

Liam hummed against my pussy and continued to bury his fingers deep as he let me ride wave after wave of pleasure. When the last of the pulses subsided, Liam gave me one more lick before he released me and sucked his digits clean.

"Can we try it without a condom? I've never done that before," I blurted before I let my brain catch up with me.

Liam's chest vibrated. "*Dulcinée*, as much as I want to, I have to protect you."

"I'm on the pill."

"*Dulcinée…*" he whined.

"What does that mean?" I stroked his jaw.

"*Dulcinée*? It means sweetheart."

He'd called me that from the very beginning. My heart soared, and I felt the prick of tears at the back of my eyes. He was the sweetest man in this entire world.

Liam retrieved his phone from his pants and dialed Duke, putting him on speaker. "Are you alone?"

"Yes. I'm out on patrol."

"Abbey has something she wants to ask. You might want to pull over." The sound of rustling came through the speakers. "Okay, darlin'. What did you want to ask?"

Liam looked at me, smirking. He wasn't going to help me. If I wanted this, I had to say it again. The butterflies in my stomach swarmed.

I took a deep breath. "I asked Liam if we could do it without a condom."

Duke moaned into the phone. "Darlin', do you know what you're asking?"

"I do, and I want to try it. I've never done it before. And I'm on the pill."

"Fuck. Hold on. I have to get out of this car." More noises came from the other end until Duke let out a breath. "Is this really what you want?"

"Yes." I didn't hesitate.

"How wet is she, Liam?" Duke growled into the phone. The vibrations hitting me straight on my sensitive clit.

Liam reached forward and swiped a finger through my folds, bringing it up glistening with my arousal. "Soaking. She's two orgasms in for the night."

"Do it." Duke's deep voice left no room for question.

"You ready for this?" Liam fisted his dick.

"Absolutely." Licking my parched lips, I nodded. Liam set the phone in the middle of the bed so Duke could hear. Shifting, he hovered over me, lining his cock with my entrance.

"Wait," I said, putting my hand on his chest. Liam froze. "Can I be on top?"

Liam and Duke groaned. "Fuck, *dulcinée*. You can do whatever you want."

I smiled, and Liam flipped to his back, pulling me on top of him. Then he scooted us until he propped against the headboard. I rocked my bare pussy on his hard length, coating it in my arousal.

"If you want me to come deep in that pussy, you'd better put me in soon, *dulcinée*. I won't be able to hold out much longer."

"Darlin', stop teasing him. Grab that big cock and sink down on it," Duke's strained voice chimed in.

"Yes, sir," I said, and Duke answered with a growl that triggered a fresh flood between my legs.

I gripped Liam's dick, placed him at my opening, and sank down, inch by inch. Liam groaned French words that licked across my skin and added to my arousal. I gasped when I was fully seated against his thighs.

"Tell Duke how it feels," he gasped.

"So big, so deep, so good," I groaned as Liam shifted his hips underneath me, making his dick hit different places. My eyes fluttered closed, and I forced them open to look at the man between my legs.

"Are you going to let Duke feel how heavenly this pussy feels?"

"As soon as he gets home." I could barely concentrate on what Liam was saying, but I knew I wanted Duke to know I wanted the same experience with him.

Muttered words filtered through the phone, followed by groaning. "Fuck him good, darlin'."

I rode Liam fast and hard, his hands gripping my hips, slamming me on his cock with each thrust. The pleasure was so intense, my head spun. I came in a blinding burst, crashing down on him and holding him deep. My head fell back, and I screamed his name as he bit into my neck. His cock swelled, and I felt the warmth of his cum splash against my walls as he came deep inside me.

Through the speaker, Duke grunted out his release. He had come to the sounds of us fucking, and it was incredibly hot. I wanted him here with us, but I knew he would be as soon as he could.

Liam nuzzled my neck, kissing and licking the sensitive skin, soothing the spot he'd just bitten.

"I promise I'll get off you when I can feel my legs again," I whimpered. My body felt weightless, and I didn't know when I'd be able to move. I loved the feeling of lying there with Liam.

"Never, *dulcinée.*" Liam wrapped his arms around my waist and held me tight as I collapsed against his chest.

"Get some rest, darlin'. I have a feeling that won't be your last orgasm tonight," Duke's voice was breathy, and I didn't know where he was, but I would have loved to watch him stroke himself to completion.

"Have a good night, Duke. I miss you already."

"Don't you worry, darlin', you won't be waiting much longer for me." He drew in a deep breath. "I miss you too."

I wanted to swoon. After the most amazing night with Liam, I got to hear Duke share his feelings with me. A tiny kernel of satisfaction grew in my chest, knowing he missed me as much as I missed him.

DUKE

*O*ver the next week, Liam and I turned the spare room into a studio for Abbey. She wasn't using it anymore, and Liam's idea had been a good one. The way her eyes lit up when we brought her into the room was more than worth it.

She had her own private space to be creative. Even with the supplies Tori had already ordered, we sat with Abbey to get everything she needed to live her dream. Some evenings, we'd find her painting late into the night, completely lost to her muse, with paint on her cheek or across her arms and fingers. It was adorable to see her doing something she loved.

When she let us see her latest masterpiece, I could hardly believe my eyes. She painted one of the paddocks with a few of the horses running through it being chased by Jax. It was incredible, and I immediately thought of a place in the house to hang it—right on the wall where the living room opened. It could be seen from at least three different rooms. She wasn't completely finished with it yet, but when she was, we'd be ready to show it off to anyone who visited.

I tried to put the fence incident behind me, but it was nearly impossible. We hadn't had any other issues since, but nothing added up. The cameras had only caught a silhouette of someone cutting the one fence that didn't have the dead heifers, but why would someone do that? King's Ranch had few enemies, and we could rule most of them out. As of now, all evidence pointed to kids cutting the fence and the deaths being an accident, but there was nothing specific pointing to that either. And it didn't help I still didn't have a report on what might have killed those heifers. The frustration of living in a small town is that toxicology reports took forever to process.

My phone beeped in my pocket. I was sprawled on the guest bed, watching Abbey's brush grace the canvas in her newest creation. It was way better than watching tv, and I got to see her face light up when her creativity was at an all-time high.

Looking at the screen, it was an urgent message from our ranch group.

Gavin: 911 in barn one.

I scrambled out of bed, and Abbey looked over her shoulder.

"Sorry, darlin'. I need to rush out." I kissed the top of her head and gave Jax a scratch between the ears.

"Is everything okay?" Her forehead scrunched, and her eyes narrowed.

"Everything's fine. I'll be back soon." I left the room, slid my shoes on at the door, and rushed out. I ran as fast as I could to barn one to see smoke rising from the north corner.

What the fuck?

Smoke billowed out the side door. Liam rushed out with Zeus, coughing and trying his best to wrangle the spooked horse.

"Get the horses," was all he could manage in a raspy voice.

I headed in, darting past Zeus' stall where there was a blaze alight in the hay.

Fuck. This was bad.

I rushed to the next stall where its occupant paced at the door, eyes wide. Grabbing the lead rope, I clipped it on the halter and threw open the door. The mare bolted out, nearly pulling my arm from its socket. I broke into a jog to the door away from the fire. As I passed the other stalls, I saw Hunter and Kyle grabbing their horses and leading them to safety.

Handing off my rescue to Kyle, I jogged back in to see Matt and Gavin grabbing water buckets from the closest stalls, throwing them on the fire. Liam pulled another horse out, and I went into the stall after he left to retrieve the water bucket. When I reached Zeus' stall, the fire was extinguished. I threw my bucket on the smoking pile of hay for good measure.

Gavin stepped into the aisle and ordered all the riders to evacuate the remaining horses and put them out in the paddocks. Everyone went from stall to stall, opening all the doors to vent the barn. Through the haze, I could see

Thomas and Declan talking to the riders as they exited with the horses in their grasp.

"Can someone please tell me how the fuck this happened?" Thomas boomed, his accent thicker with his rage.

"No one noticed anything until it was too late. When we heard the horses going crazy, we rushed out, and the fire was already ablaze," Liam choked out, then coughed. "It was isolated to Zeus' stall. We caught it before it could spread."

Thomas' jaw tightened, but he went to Liam and placed a hand on his shoulder. "Did you bring him to Caleb for a look?"

Liam nodded. "I left him with Caleb." He'd taken him straight to our resident equine vet. I wanted Caleb to do a thorough checkup to make sure he hadn't gotten injured in any way.

I caught Liam's gaze, and he nodded. He'd gotten to his horse in time. I let out a deep breath and marched into the stall. I wanted to find out what had happened, and the best way to do that was to see the starting point. Hopefully, there would be clues to tell us what had gone wrong.

I'd just stepped into the stall when I froze. There was a blackened patch of hay where the fire was and written above it on the wall in a jagged, angry scrawl were the words:

She's mine. I want her back.

Gavin peered around me and muttered under his

breath. I stepped farther into the stall, letting more people in.

"Who is *she?*" Matt asked.

"A horse? A rider? There are a lot of possibilities." Declan came around the outside of the stall with a few others.

"Do we think the fire could have been an accident?" Kyle, the most optimistic of the group, asked.

"No. I think this was done intentionally. Look at this." Gavin bent over and picked up a half-burned pack of cigarettes.

"No one here smokes." Matt's forehead creased.

"How did that get in here? And how did no one smell it?" Thomas growled through clenched teeth. "It's the late afternoon, people. How did we not see this?"

"Someone must have snuck in, lit the cigarettes, and set it aside. It was like a ticking time-bomb. It doesn't take long for hot ashes to light hay on fire." I rubbed the back of my neck. While it wasn't difficult to set a fire this way, we needed to know if it was deliberate or an accident.

Hunter jogged to us as I finished talking. "I think it was deliberate. I was walking the perimeter and found the hose cut straight through. Someone made sure it would be harder for us to put out the fire." Hunter came around to stand next to Declan.

Declan slammed a fist on the edge of a stall. "Who would fucking do this?"

"Duke, can you grab the video surveillance for this area and let us know if you find something?" Thomas asked before turning to Hunter. "How are all the horses?"

"Caleb just finished an initial once over. Everyone

looks okay for now, except for a cut on Atlas' leg, but he doesn't think Atlas will need stitches." The tension in the stall seemed to dissipate slightly.

"It was a good thing half the horses are turned out right now. It could have been worse," Kyle said, a relieved look on his face.

"Let's get this place aired out. Any fans lying around, bring them in here. Duke, do what you need to do with Zeus' stall so we can get it cleaned and freshened up for him," Thomas ordered.

"Do you want us to keep this from the girls?" Gavin rubbed the back of his neck.

"Yes. Especially because of the note. I don't want to worry any of them." Thomas pinched the bridge of his nose.

"I have a theory." Hunter stepped forward. "Do you think it could be about Grace?"

"Grace?" Gavin's fists clenched and unclenched at his side. The mention of his sister-in-law being in trouble had him tensing.

"Just think about it. Her old trainer was a jerk. He left Grace only to have her sign on with us. She immediately soared to the top and won Olympic gold. She said he had a temper. Maybe this is a twisted way of scaring her into coming back and training with him. He seems like a glory hog and would do just about anything to see his name in the spotlight."

Liam nodded at Hunter's logic, while Gavin ran a hand down his face. It made sense.

"Why start a fire?" I paced the small space, trying to wrap my head around the situation.

"It was in Liam's stall. You think he wanted to take out her competition? Liam did go with her and won medals too," Matt pipped in.

"Those are good theories," I said. "I'll gather what I can and bring it in. I'll see how quickly I can get people out here—"

"No. I don't want anyone out here. I need you to figure out what you can without anything getting out, Duke. I can't have the ranch under investigation or have a bunch of people disturbing our day to day. We just landed a new sponsor and news of this could have them pulling out." Thomas' hand sliced through the air.

Declan stepped up next to his brother. "I agree. Do what you can, Duke. I'll have Mikel look into Grace's old trainer and see if we can get his whereabouts over the last few weeks. Let us know when you've combed through the camera footage from this week and see if you catch anything suspicious. Come straight to us if you do."

I nodded. It went against all my training not to report this, but Thomas and Declan were my bosses, and I followed their orders. I didn't want this getting out either, but I knew it would turn serious if we didn't do something fast. Two weeks ago, Declan lost two of his breeders, and today we could have lost competing horses. Now we knew someone was after one of the girls. Hunter had a reasonable explanation for it being Grace, but my gut said we were missing something.

"Everyone clear out of the stall and let me see what I can come up with. Liam, grab my camera from the house and meet me back here. I want you to tell me if something looks off. Matt, I want you to go around the perimeter and do the same. Same goes for you, Gavin. Comb through this barn," I dished out orders and started pushing people out of the stall. I'd treat this like a crime scene the best I could, since they didn't want anyone else involved. It wouldn't be the best, having so many people walk through it, but it would do well enough.

Everyone in the vicinity was given a task, and when I was finally alone, my chest tightened. I rushed out the back door to get much-needed fresh air. The smokey barn was making it hard to breathe on top of the heavy feeling settling on my shoulders and chest.

It was my job to keep this place safe, and twice I'd failed this month. How had this happened and who was targeting us? We had created a safe space for everyone here, and we took security seriously. The ranch was far away from the nearest neighbor, and we kept to ourselves.

Leaning on the fence, I rested my forehead on my forearms. The smoke seemed to follow me, but at least I wasn't in the confined stall, sucking it in. I could breathe easier. I closed my eyes and tilted my head toward the sky, letting the warmth of the sun seep in. The October breeze hit my face, trying its best to calm me, but the fear continued to build in my heart.

"I know that look. You can't blame yourself." Liam's voice wafted over to me. I opened my eyes and noticed his slow approach from the fence on the other side of me.

I rolled my neck and winced at how tight it was. "How is it *not* my fault? What is it I do here? I'm the head of security for the ranch, and we've had two incidents in the last week."

"These are hardly normal incidents, and you know it." He arched his eyebrow. "*Mon pote*, you know no one is thinking you didn't do your job."

I groaned. "I should have known something was happening."

"Unless you just became psychic, how would you have known?" Liam pushed back on my thinking.

"Liam…"

"Duke. You had everything in place that you needed to do your job. Now at least you can use those tools, like the cameras, to see if there are additional clues."

I nodded and let out a heavy sigh.

Liam patted me on the back. "No one here blames you, and no one would want to see you beating yourself up about this."

I ignored him. A part of me couldn't fully believe what he was saying. "Did you check on Abbey?" I was hyper alert and wanted to be sure she was safe.

"Yes, she was painting when I stopped in," Liam answered.

"Good. She can't find out," I rasped.

"She's going to at some point," Liam reminded me.

"Right, and I want to have answers by then. We're keeping her in the dark for now. Or better yet, maybe she shouldn't be here. If I can't protect our ranch, what makes you think I can protect her and you? Maybe she should leave." I pushed from the fence. Taking a deep breath, I forced myself to ignore the blood pounding in my ears and regain control over my breathing before it was too late. Without another word, I grabbed the camera bag from him.

"You don't mean that, Duke. It's just your fear talking. While this is scary, you need to have more faith in her... and in us." Liam followed me.

"Of course it's fear talking. Do you want me to tell you it wouldn't destroy me if something happened to the woman I love or anyone else on this ranch? It's my *job* to keep everyone safe." I stopped short. I replayed the words. *Love.* I'd just admitted I loved Abbey.

"No, Duke. I want you to admit it will. You are just like the rest of us, with fears and emotions."

I sighed and put the camera together. We'd had this argument many times before. He wanted me to admit to *all* the emotions racing through me, but he didn't know I never suppressed them. I just hid them so I could be what everyone else needed. If I let my fears rule me, there was no way I'd keep anyone safe. It's why I had to lock them down.

"Comb through Zeus' stall and let me know if you see anything out of place." I pointed to the door, and Liam climbed the fence to join me. I snapped pictures of everything I could find. The burned hay pile, the message, the cigarette pack, the cut hose, and a pair of garden clippers Matt found nearby.

If I'd been running this through the town's police force, I'd have numbered each piece of evidence, but since it was just for us, I didn't bother. I bagged everything I could, even though the Kingstons didn't want a formal investigation. It was frustrating we didn't have any foot-prints I could try to match. Too many people had run in and out of the stall before we realized it might be a crime scene. And there were likely multiple fingerprints on the stall that would be hard to weed out if the culprit left any behind without the proper devices to catalog and identify each one.

At least I would have some evidence to use as clues about the vandal's identity.

When I finished, I left Liam to finish cleaning out the stall with instructions to call me if he found anything else. In Gavin's office, I downloaded videos from all the cameras around the ranch. I was going to watch every video as many times as I needed to make sure I didn't miss anything.

Back at the house, I went straight to my office and plugged in the drive. I went through the cameras that would have had the least activity on them and didn't find anything out of the ordinary.

The next ones I loaded were the main ones from outside and inside the barn. I was grateful I'd insisted we needed cameras in both places. The upcoming days had nothing unusual until I came to the day before. We'd had multiple deliveries according to Gavin, but none of the drivers ever stepped foot in the barn. They always unloaded outside, and Matt and his crew would bring everything in.

This time, there was a tall, thin man who entered the barn and walked up and down the aisle. He didn't touch anything, he just looked around. His hat shielded his face, and he was wearing jeans and a basic t-shirt he could have purchased at any big-box general retailer. He easily blended in with everyone else working the ranch.

I continued watching, coming up to the last few hours. The guy came back today. The timestamp indicated he'd been there only thirty minutes before the fire started. He still covered his face, but this time, when he came in, he went immediately into the camera's blind spot, and a few minutes later, the camera went dead.

Son of a bitch! He had been scouting the barn the day before so he could take out the damn cameras. I slammed my fist on my desk, causing everything to rattle with the force. I pulled up another angle of the barn, but it hadn't caught anything useful.

My blood went cold, and I fought against a wave of panic that threatened to overtake me. I still had a few more cameras to look at, but the only real clue we had was effectively useless. No one could identify the guy based on what the camera had caught.

A rap on the door made me jump in my chair. Liam froze when he saw me. Suddenly, my vision tunneled, and it was harder and harder to breathe. Liam crouched so his face was even with mine. "Duke. Are you with me?" His hand weighed on my shoulder. His presence settled me, but not as much as Abbey's had during the last episodes.

"I'm fine," I growled and tried pushing his hand away, even knowing I couldn't fool him. I'd calmed myself enough that his worried gaze pissed me off. I was *fine…* or at least I would be in a few minutes.

"Did you find anything?" His tone was gentle.

"Yes," I snapped, hating the way he treated me—like I was about to fall apart. I drew in a breath and let it out slowly. "But it's a dead end. The guy cut the video feed. Can't get a good view of him."

"Dammit." Liam rubbed his forehead. "What do we do?"

"I'm going to take a look at the feed again and see if I missed anything." I'd no sooner gotten out the words than my chest tightened, and I began to pant. What if I couldn't keep everyone safe? What if next time someone got hurt or died? I couldn't have that on my watch again.

Liam took one look at me. "I'm going to go find Abbey." He stood and strode to the door.

"No," my voice boomed in the small space. "I can't see her right now." I couldn't. I didn't want her to see me fall apart *again*. This was the worst I'd been in a long time. So many episodes so close together were wearing on me, and I didn't want to scare her.

"I think she's exactly what you need. Don't fight this. Let her help you."

"I'm going to take a shower." I shoved my way past him and went to my room. As the water heated, I stripped and stepped under the spray. It was enough to calm my emotions for me to handle them, but I still couldn't settle the unease churning in my stomach.

I needed to protect Abbey, and someone had gotten close enough to set fire to the barn. What if she'd been in there? What if she had gotten in the way of the guy on accident? Would he have done something to harm her? I'd never forgive myself if something happened to her.

"Duke?" Abbey's voice filtered in through the open door.

I looked up and groaned as she entered the room. I was going to kill Liam for not heeding my demands.

"Liam told me I'd find you in here." The worry in her voice was like a knife to my heart.

I couldn't pull my gaze away from hers, no matter how much I tried.

"Oh, Duke," she crooned at what she saw in my eyes.

She opened the shower door and cupped my cheek.

I reached for her without thinking and pulled her in with me, clothes and all. Liam was right; I did need her. I needed to know she was here, she was safe, and she was mine. I needed to feel her, fuck her.

I crushed my lips against hers. Her hands gripped the back of my head and neck, and she kissed me with such ferocity, it was like she knew the turmoil raging inside me. I pushed her against the wall and rid her of her shirt. When her pants and panties were on the other side of the shower, I hauled her up until she wrapped her legs around my waist.

She brushed her hand over my dripping hair and nodded at the silent request I was giving her. That was all I needed. I slid into her with one solid thrust. She gasped, and I groaned. Her pussy gripped my cock as I slowly retreated, then surged forward. I fucked Abbey hard and fast. She hung on and took everything I had to give her, coming so beautifully, it pushed me over the edge.

I leaned my forehead against hers and let the water spray over us as we both came down from the rush.

"I'm so sorry. Did I hurt you?" I looked at her, realizing I'd never taken her that hard before.

"I won't break, Duke." Abbey kissed me. She didn't let go until the muscles in my body relaxed.

When I released her, we scrubbed each other's bodies. She had some special power over me, and I wanted her to be mine forever.

ABBEY

"*A*bbey, you have to wear that. You look totally hot in it," Grace said as she admired me in the dress she loaned me.

"No, I can't." I tugged at the hem. It was shorter than anything I'd ever worn, and it clung to my body like a second skin.

"What? Why not? That dress totally screams you." Blake stood beside me at the mirror in the guest room in the big house where we were all getting ready. "You look beautiful."

I blew out a heavy sigh. "Jeff would never let me out of the house wearing something like this. He would think I was wearing it to piss him off." My voice broke. I'd only worn a dress like this once with him, and I regretted how small he made me feel once we got home and he could yell at me in private.

It was still hard to get over the things he did to me or commanded I do. He never let me wear anything too revealing and always found reasons why I shouldn't go out for a girl's night. Everything about this outing felt foreign.

"Abbey, honey. You are no longer with Jeff." Grace wrapped an arm around my shoulder. "You're a free woman. You can do whatever you want now. Including wearing that hot dress." Grace gently reminded me. Her words settled in my chest, creating a warm feeling inside me. It was a good thing I'd fled to the ranch on instinct. Being around Blake and Grace would help me recover so much faster and gain that feminine confidence back.

I twisted my hands together. I heard what they were saying, but what if tonight was just like that other night? "I don't want to upset Liam and Duke. I don't want them thinking I'm wearing this to get attention from the other guys. I can't do that to them. I can't take that chance." They were already so good to me. I didn't want to ruin it over a stupid dress.

"Abbey," Blake said, but I couldn't look at her. I was afraid if I did, I might tear up.

I tugged frantically at the zipper, needing to get changed before the guys saw me. "I'll just wear what I was going to. This dress is gorgeous, Grace, but I can't." My voice broke. "I just can't." I wanted to be able to wear whatever I wanted to make me feel good, sexy, confident, and special. But the fear had lodged itself so deep inside of me I didn't know when that might ever happen.

"Come on, Abbs. You *have* to wear this. The guys are going to love it. You already know they are *nothing* like Jeff," Grace pleaded.

A light rapping on the door ended our conversation. "Everyone decent?" Duke called through the door.

Everyone around me laughed and scrambled to cover up. Victoria finally answered, "Yes, come on in."

I froze. My breathing sped up, and my heart beat wildly in my chest. Duke was about to see me.

He opened the door, and the moment his gaze found mine, I dropped my eyes to the floor. I was afraid to see the anger on his face.

The room quieted until it was practically silent. I stood where I was until his boots appeared on the floor in front of me. His finger slipped under my chin, and he lifted my face to meet his. "Darlin', what's going on?"

I shook my head. Fear clogged my throat.

He patiently waited, his thumb rubbing back and forth in a soothing motion.

I bit my lip. "I was just about to change."

His expression remained the same, and the anger I expected didn't appear. He let go of my chin. "Why would you do that?"

My shoulders dropped, and my face fell. I knew this was a disaster waiting to happen. It was only a matter of time before he got angry. "It's too much." I brushed my hand along the front of Grace's little black strapless dress.

He shook his head. "I'm half tempted to not let you leave the house looking like that," his low voice rumbled. I dropped my eyes to the floor again. He caught my chin between his fingers and forced me to look at him. "I said *half* tempted. You deserve to go out and have a good time with the girls in this dress that only adds to your beauty."

My heart soared. I let out a shaky breath and gave him

a trembling smile. He really was okay with letting me go dressed like this. I wouldn't let him regret it. "I promise not to do anything bad. I won't look at or flirt with another guy. I promise I won't have too much fun or drink too much. I won't—"

He pressed a finger to my lips and chuckled. "Have fun, darlin'. You need it. I appreciate knowing you won't be flirting with other men because you're mine and Liam's. Dance, drink. I trust you, and I trust these girls will make sure you have a good time. Just know that Liam and I will be waiting for you to come back so we can enjoy you in *and* out of this dress."

The giggling from the girls sounded so faint compared to the blood pounding in my ears. I licked my lips, and Duke's eyes traced every movement. His words of trust only enhanced the desire coursing through my veins for him.

"It would be rude to ask the girls to leave the room so I could have my way with you right now, so I'd better leave before I get myself into trouble." Duke placed a searing kiss to my lips. He adjusted himself, not even bothering to hide his actions, then turned to leave. "Heels. She needs some heels," Duke said as he strolled out the door, leaving the girls staring at me.

"I told you so." Grace bumped my shoulder and finished getting dressed.

For the first time in as long as I could remember, I was looking forward to going out. Tonight was going to be so much fun. We were celebrating Alex's approaching wedding, even though this wasn't her official bachelorette party. Blake was about to pop, and poor Victoria was getting almost too big to get around comfortably. Those twins were growing quickly. They all wanted to go out and have some fun while they still could.

When everyone was ready, we filed out to say our goodbyes to the men, who were all watching football in the living room. It took everything for Blake to stop Gavin and Travis from messing up her makeup. Caleb and Andrew were fawning over Tori's getup. Jessie, Grace, and Alex handled their men well, but I could only focus on Liam and Duke.

Duke's smile warmed my heart, while Liam's devilish grin ignited my soul.

"Oh, I can't wait to rip that dress off you when you get home tonight," Liam growled.

"Gently, please. I want that dress back in one piece." Grace winked.

"You can have the dress. I want Abbey in nothing but those heels," Duke purred.

I squirmed between them. "You can have me however you want when we get home."

"Then we'd better let you girls get going. The sooner you leave, the sooner you'll be back." Liam stepped back and escorted me to the car. We climbed into the back of the limo and greeted Martin, our driver.

"Ladies," he said in return through the window dividing the front from the back. "Champagne and sparkling cider are in the chiller. I should have you to Amarillo in an hour and a half."

"Thank you, Martin," we all said in unison, then laughed.

The drive to Amarillo went by quickly with the cham-

171

pagne and cider keeping us occupied. We stopped for dinner and then went to the clubs. Before I knew it, I was buzzed and having the best time of my life. I just wished Liam and Duke were here so I could dance with them. Blake and Tori had to sit out most of the time, but Alex and Grace were my partners on the dance floor.

"Be right back, ladies. I have to go to the bathroom." I tossed back my shot at the table and looked for the nearest restroom sign.

"Do you want us to come with you?" Jessie asked, taking a sip of her fruity cocktail.

"I'll be fine." I headed to the back corner and waited in line.

"Excuse me." The deep voice coming from behind me had ice settling in my veins. *Jeff?* I scanned the crowd in search of the owner but found only other girls waiting in line.

When I didn't see anyone familiar, I took a deep breath to calm my nerves. It had to have been my imagination. I was having too much fun, and I was feeling good from the alcohol. My mind had to be sabotaging my good time.

When it was my turn, I went as quickly as possible. I wanted to return to the safety of the girls as soon as I could. Next time, I'd be sure to take Jessie's offer to have someone come with me.

On my way back, I heard the voice again. "You think you can leave me that easily?"

The anger resonating in each word made me stop in my tracks. I spun in place, looking for the source, and spotted a man weaving through the bodies who looked very similar to Jeff from the back.

The instinct to run screamed at me, and I bumped into someone. "I'm so sorry," I said to the gentleman who gave me an annoyed glance before returning to his friends.

I needed to calm down. There was no way Jeff could be here. I was in the middle of Texas. It'd been weeks since I left him. I hadn't returned any of his calls or texts. How could he possibly know where I was?

Either way, the anxiety racing through my veins had me pushing my way through the crowd, bumping into one person after the other. I looked around and caught a glimpse of a face that resembled Jeff. Choking down a scream, I hurried to the table where the girls were waiting.

"Abbey, are you okay?" Grace asked, putting a hand on my arm.

"I swear I'm seeing Jeff," I gasped.

"Honey, there's no way he'd be here." Blake's calm voice reminded me how crazy I was being.

"You're right. I know you're right. But I keep hearing his voice, and I saw someone in the crowd who looked just like him." I cringed and couldn't help looking over my shoulder.

"Okay, let's get you some water. Maybe that would help you calm down." Jessie flagged down the bartender.

"And maybe we should call it a night anyway. It's late, and we still have a long drive home," Tori added.

"I didn't mean to ruin the night," I whispered. Tears still clogged my throat, and the terror I'd felt still hadn't subsided.

"Abbs, you aren't ruining anything. It's one in the morning. We've been out all night and had a good time." Blake flashed her phone screen at me. She was right. We hadn't planned on being out this late, but we'd gotten caught up in the night.

"We're all going to feel it in the morning." Alex winced. I pulled my phone from my clutch and saw a text from Duke making sure we were still okay. Tapping a quick reply, I let him know we were hailing Martin and heading home.

Martin had the limo pulled up out front for us. Gripping each other, we all stumbled out the door and packed into the car. I took one last glance behind us as we pulled away, and I could have sworn I saw Jeff standing on the corner of the street. I turned around quickly and forced myself to forget about it. It had to be my thoughts from earlier in the evening messing with me... or the alcohol.

The girls were right. Jeff was in Georgia, in our apartment, probably fucking that same woman. I sighed and settled into my seat. We laughed and chatted for a half hour or so before we all quieted down. Blake and Tori were the first ones to pass out. We may have been out to have fun, but we weren't in our early teens anymore.

I finally gave in to sleep as the late night and adrenaline surge exhausted me.

* * *

EVERYWHERE I LOOKED, there was Jeff.

I turned and ran to another room, but he was in there

174

too. He was in every room I tried. No matter which direction I turned, Jeff popped up out of nowhere.

He drew closer each time he came into view. My heart was pounding so loud I swore it was going to beat out of my chest. Blood rushed through me and pounded in my eardrums.

I raced from room to room, unable to find the way out. Fear had taken over, and I was sobbing. I ran down the next corridor, finally losing sight of him. I prayed I'd escaped and hoped to find someone I knew who could help me.

In the next room, I collided with a hard body, knocking me backward. I fell to the ground and scrambled away. When I looked up, my breath seized in my chest and came in short pants as I crawled away as fast as I could. It was Jeff. He was right here, and I couldn't get away.

Even though there were other people in the room, no one paid me any attention. How could they not see I was trying to escape? Why wouldn't they help? I scrambled to my feet and raced around the next corner, only to find Jeff blocking my path.

He grabbed me by my hair, hauling me up in front of him. Pain seared through my scalp and fear locked my limbs in place.

"Bitch, you think you can run away from me?"

I tried to scream, but nothing came out.

"You can never get rid of me. You are mine."

I struggled in his tight grasp, but I couldn't get free. Jeff's hand reached out and wrapped around my throat. I gasped for air, but I could barely suck in a breath. He was going to kill me.

"I will find you. No matter where you run."

My body thrashed, trying to buck him off me. I swung my fist, the lack of oxygen already making my movements slower. I clawed at my throat, but his hand wouldn't release me. I looked into his eyes and saw the anger raging in them. His free hand swiped for a strike I remembered all too well. When the blow hit my cheek, I screamed.

"Abbey, darlin'. Wake up." Duke's voice penetrated through my thoughts, and I jolted awake.

I still couldn't catch my breath. It felt like I was still drowning in fear. My cheek burned from the memory.

"Dulcinée, it's okay. It was only a dream. You're safe. You're here with us." Liam's French accent washed over me, and my head cleared.

Duke was on the other side of me. His hands gently stroked my face, soothing the imaginary sting from the dream. "Look at me, darlin'."

I pried my eyes open and saw Duke hovering over me. Worry etched over every line of his face. My heart ached knowing I had put that there. He brushed my hair from my sweat-soaked face. "Breathe with me, Abbey."

I locked eyes with him. He breathed in, and so did I. Then he let his breath out slowly, and I let my breath match his. We continued until my chest loosened, and I didn't feel like I was going to pass out.

"There you are." Liam eased into view beside Duke.

"I'm sorry. I didn't mean to…" I could find the words to express the terror that tugged at me even now.

"You're apologizing for having a bad dream? *Dulcinée,* you can't help it." Liam pulled me against his chest.

"I thought I was supposed to be the one with the nightmares." Duke smiled, and I felt my heart skip. He stroked my hair and asked me what my dream was about, but I shook my head. I wasn't ready to tell them. Not yet, at least.

"I didn't mean to wake you. I'm sorry." I let out a deep breath. The nightmare was over, and Jeff was nowhere near me. I was safe in bed with Duke and Liam. Between them, right where I belonged.

"We want to make sure that you're okay. Whatever you need, we're here for you," Duke whispered, and I sighed. Eventually, Duke tucked me close to his side, and Liam took over the calm strokes along my body until heat licked through my veins, taking away the chill from the dream.

"Now that we're awake, let's show you how much we missed you tonight." Liam kissed my temple, then worked his way down my neck and chest. My *bare* chest. I was naked.

The last thing I remembered was falling asleep in the limo with the girls. The more I thought about it, I vaguely remembered forcing my eyes open as they lifted me from the car. And Liam's gentle kiss on my forehead before I fell back asleep.

The giddiness inside me rose, knowing they carried me from the car, stripped me down, knowing I liked to sleep with nothing on, and put me to bed.

"Please," I begged. "Please show me how much you missed me, because I missed you both so much."

With Liam's lips caressing my stomach, I pulled Duke to me and kissed him. This was where I wanted to be. Just like I had helped make Duke's nightmares go away, so had these two with mine. With just their touches, I imagined a new future with them—one where I didn't have anything to worry about.

LIAM

I swallowed hard, remembering the terror on Abbey's face when she woke the night before. I'd seen it so many times with Duke, but it broke my heart knowing I couldn't help Abbey with hers. I'd woken up when she started tossing and moaning, but not knowing what the dream stemmed from, I hesitated to wake her in case I made it worse.

I spent most of the next day watching for any signs that she had any lingering effects from it like Duke sometimes did. We went to the barn, and she helped groom Zeus with me. She watched us as I gave him a workout and then assisted me when I had to give him a bath.

Duke joined us in the paddocks, bringing a picnic lunch and her sketchbook so she could draw while we lay under the tree where I'd first met her. When she shyly turned her book around, I noticed she'd drawn Duke against the tree and me lying in the grass. She hadn't said she loved us yet, but in each stroke of her pencil, I could see her love shining through. We just needed to give her more time.

Abbey cooked the Bolognese dinner she'd been planning. She let me be her sous chef, and I let her boss me around the kitchen. I didn't even try to hide my raging hard-on. It was hot having her take charge.

After dinner, we retired to the living room and turned on a movie. Halfway through, Abbey got up and took our empty whiskey glasses with her to the cabinet where we stashed the liquor.

"What are you doing, darlin'?" Duke's voice rumbled.

Abbey flinched and froze in place. "Refilling your glasses." Her voice sounded nothing like her confident self.

"*Dulcinée*, you don't have to do that. We should be taking care of you. Would you like another glass of wine?" I motioned for her to come back to us.

Abbey shook her head. "No, thank you. I shouldn't have had the first one. I'll pour you both another and be right there." She took a step toward the liquor cabinet.

"Darlin', we don't need another. What we need is you." The crease in Duke's brows grew deeper. We both could sense there was something else happening.

Abbey stood still, not looking at either of us. Her hands trembled, making the glasses shake. I glanced at Duke, and he met my gaze. Something was off, and it was time to find out what.

"Abbey, sit down." Duke patted the space between us. "We need to have a heart to heart."

When she didn't come over right away, I stood,

relieved her of the glasses, and led her to the couch. Her bewildered gaze met mine, as though she didn't know how she'd gotten back here. "We need to know everything. I noticed the bruises marring your skin when you first got here, and you seem jumpy. You had a nightmare after what was supposed to be a fun girl's night. What's going on?"

"We don't have any secrets around here, darlin'. Tell us what's wrong. We can't help if we don't know."

"I don't know how to tell you." Her eyes were glued to her hands in her lap. "I don't want you to think less of me."

"Oh darlin', we could never think less of you."

"Start with something simple," I suggested.

She stayed silent, her eyes rapidly blinking away tears.

My heart wrenched, and I couldn't speak seeing her so distraught.

"Let's start at the beginning," Duke said in a soothing tone. "When I found you on the side of the road, the girls didn't know you were coming. What made you leave so suddenly you didn't have time to tell them?"

Her body trembled. I wanted to reach out to her, but Duke shook his head. We needed to give her space.

She bit her lip. Her voice was so low I had to strain to hear her. "I left my ex. I'd been trying to leave him for a while, but I couldn't get away. He never let me out of his sight. But for once, he agreed I could visit my mother. I can't remember the last time he let me go anywhere alone."

The defeat in her voice just about killed me. I had to

clench and unclench my hands by my side. I wanted to reach out and hit something.

Abbey took a deep breath. "When I came home early from my trip, I found him in our bed with another woman. It was the wake up call I needed. He didn't care about me. I don't think he ever did."

"Son of a bitch." I couldn't help it. How could anyone cheat on my beautiful *dulcinée*? This guy was a fucking asshole.

Her face snapped to mine.

I hated the surprise that skittered across her face. The fact that he created any doubt in her mind that she was less than perfect had anger firing through me.

"I left him and ran here. Grace and Blake had been trying to get me to leave him for years, but I couldn't. I'd grown blind to the way he'd treated me. I'd come to expect it—to think everything was my fault. That I didn't deserve anyone better than him." Her voice sounded so small. If I ever found that bastard, I was going to kill him.

"What happened after that?" Duke asked.

"What do you mean? That was it. I came here." She looked from Duke to me, not understanding where he was going with his question.

"How did he take the breakup?" I clarified. I wanted to know just as much as Duke did.

"Not very well, according to the texts and messages on my old phone. After the first few, I couldn't look or listen to them anymore. They just kept piling up with no cell service. I shut my phone off and tried to forget about it." Tears escaped and rolled down her cheeks.

I leaned over and gently brushed them away. She

sniffed and gave me a tiny smile of thanks. When I pulled my hand back, she thread her fingers through mine. I held on tight, not ever wanting to let go.

"Was the nightmare about him?" Duke's voice grew darker.

"Yes." She gave a hiccupping sigh. "When we went to the club, I swear I saw and heard him there, but that was impossible. He doesn't even know I'm at King's Ranch. But my imagination went wild last night, and I dreamed of him chasing and catching me."

"Why does he scare you? What did he do before you left him?" Duke's jaw tightened. I had to hope he wasn't imagining the same things I was. The bruises. My heart tore before I heard her answer.

"He was abusive," Abbey choked out, and Duke's growl echoed around the living room. No. Not Duke's. *Mine.* I had to be careful not to crush her hand resting within my own. Anger built up inside me to a level I'd never experienced before. The bastard hit my woman.

Duke rubbed her thigh. Abbey set her hand on top of his.

"We were high school sweethearts. During school, he was sweet and flattering. But once we graduated and moved in together, things changed. He wasn't happy I was going to classes and getting a degree. It got worse when we graduated. He wanted me to stay home all day and be there when he came home from his job, but that wasn't me. Eventually, he forbid me from seeing people and going places." Abbey's head fell forward, and her voice grew thick.

"The first time he hit me was when I went to see a

friend. He was upset, and he hit me." Abbey wiped away the tears, and I hated we were making her relive these horrible moments.

"He apologized and treated me well for a month or so, then everything went back to the way it was before. Another slap for doing something he didn't like, another apology. Eventually, he got smart and did other things. Pushed me into a chair so it jabbed my ribs, tripped me so I fell hard on my knees... The bruises were in places no one could see."

"Those were the bruises I saw on your legs that first day?" Duke asked, his voice tight. I knew he was blaming himself just as much as I was, feeling the guilt that we hadn't asked about them.

"Yes. I fought to see my mother again—planned a trip to see her for a week, and he got angry. If I had asked him before, he would have said no. So, I planned it without his permission and told him after. He didn't like that there was nothing he could do about it except punish me. He knew my mother would be suspicious if I canceled."

"Why didn't you leave him before?" I asked, hoping she knew I wasn't blaming her.

"I was too scared. I knew he would track me down if I ever left him. Every time I tried to go anywhere, he showed up and ruined everything. Eventually, my friends stopped inviting me out. Blake and Grace were the only ones who knew Jeff's bad side. They don't know every-thing, even though they've been with me since I was little. They saw how he was growing up and how he became more controlling."

"I'm glad you have them on your side," I said, grateful Abbey had them in her life.

"I was getting ready to leave him. I didn't like what I'd become—a shell of a person. He wouldn't let me think or do anything for myself. I was his puppet. I didn't want that anymore. After seeing my mother, I wanted to ask Blake to come get me, but when I walked in on him, I was done. I wrote him a note and left."

"I don't think he's going to let you go that easily." I rubbed the back of my neck. I didn't want to scare her any further, but she had to be prepared. "A person like him isn't going to walk away."

"You said you've had your phone off for a while now?" Duke's eyebrows knitted together.

"I haven't turned it on since we got the new one. Why?" Abbey's head tilted to the side as she swiped at her tears.

"Who have you told that you're here?"

I had to wonder where Duke was going with these questions, but I knew his police brain was working every angle.

"Only my mother. I called her on the way home from town that day and gave her my new number."

"Does your mother know how bad Jeff is?" Duke asked.

"I've kept her in the dark about it. I didn't want her to worry or for her to get hurt. Jeff was unpredictable. I didn't know if he would try something if she tried to help me."

Duke turned his intense gaze toward me. He didn't

even have to say the words out loud. I already knew he was thinking about the message in the barn.

She's mine. I want her back.

Oh fuck.

He thought Jeff was the culprit for the fire. "*Dulcinée,* do you think your mother would have given Jeff any information about where you were or your new number?"

"I don't know. Maybe, if he called her..." She shrugged.

"I think you need to make sure. If she did, then we might have a problem." Duke's voice lowered an octave.

I could see the gears turning in Duke's head. He was already working out how Jeff fit in with everything that had happened so far.

"What kind of problem?" Her forehead creased.

"One we will deal with if it's true." Duke grabbed her cell from the table and handed it to her. She quickly dialed, and we heard the phone pick up on the second ring. Abbey tapped at her phone, activating the speaker button.

"Hi, Mom."

"Hi, sweetie. You're calling so late. Is everything okay?" her mother asked.

"Yes, Mom. I was just wondering if you'd spoken to Jeff lately. Did you tell him where I was?" Abbey's voice was shaky, but she did her best to sound as calm as she could.

"Well, yes." The confusion in her voice was heartbreaking. She had no clue what she had done to her daughter. "He was worried about you. He said he couldn't get in touch with you and was scared something had happened. I told him you went to see the girls after you left, and you had to get a temporary new number because of the signal issue. Is everything all right?"

"Everything is fine. I just needed to know. I'll call you in a few days. Love you." Abbey hung up before her mother could ask any more questions.

Her eyes were wide, and the color was slowly draining from her face.

"It's going to be okay, *dulcinée*." I scooped Abbey into my lap. She buried her face in my neck, and I felt her whole body shake. I stroked her back, and Duke scooted closer.

"Darlin', I'm going to need all the information you have on Jeff. His full name, address, phone number, and anything else you can give us. We won't let that bastard anywhere near you." He placed a hand on her knee.

Abbey looked up. "I can get you everything you need."

"Good. And I'm going to need your cell. The old one."

Abbey winced.

"Darlin', I need to see what kind of messages he's been leaving. It'll help with the restraining order."

"But—"

"It's happening," I said firmly.

"Okay." Abbey looked down, and I forced her to look at me. I hated the fear in her eyes.

"We will protect you. This is for the best." I kissed her nose, and she sighed.

"Does this mean there's a problem? You said there could be a problem." She glanced at Duke.

"Possibly. I have to check on a few things, but even if it

is, we'll handle it. That's our job. You are our woman, and no one is going to fuck with that," Duke said through gritted teeth.

"Now, let's get a few things straight." I lifted Abbey and deposited her in my spot, kneeling in front of her, happy when Duke knelt beside me. "We may be protective. We may be possessive at times, but we will *never* be like him."

"We want what's best for you, and we want to see you shine like the diamond you are. We will handle any of your problems, no matter what, because we love you, and we won't let anything happen to you." Duke cupped her cheek, and Abbey leaned into his touch.

"You love me?" Her eyes shone when she looked between the two of us.

"I love you, *dulcinée*. You complete us. You're everything we've ever wanted and more." I cupped her other cheek, needing to touch her as I confessed my love. "Since I saw you under that tree with Zeus and Jax, you've had my heart."

Duke stroked her cheekbone with his thumb, drawing her attention. "How could we not fall in love with you? You are this ray of sunshine that never ceases to shine its light right into my soul. I'm addicted to the way you make me feel, darlin'. For the first time in a long while, I feel whole again. I want to do the same for you. You are so strong, and I admire the hell out of it. I didn't want to admit it, but I think I fell in love with you that first night over pizza and football." Duke smiled.

"I love you both too. I've never felt this way before. The two of you make me feel like I can do anything, be anything, have anything I want. I love that you want me to shine when I've been in the dark for so long. I hope I can make you both as happy as you make me."

Tears swam in her eyes, and Duke surged forward to kiss her.

My heart nearly leapt out of my chest. I'd waited years to find someone special enough to call ours, but I couldn't believe it ended up being the person I'd known about for so long and never met. She was perfect for us, and I couldn't wait to start living a life with her. We just had to figure some things out first.

I couldn't wait any longer and pushed Duke to the side. They both laughed, but I didn't care. I wanted to kiss my woman and celebrate our love. When my lips claimed hers, I felt my soul ignite with passion. Kissing her wasn't enough, and I knew Duke had the same feeling. We needed to claim her, body and soul, before we were satisfied.

"Will you tell me what this other problem is?" Abbey breathed when I released her.

"Only after I confirm everything. I promise." Duke's voice was the softest I'd ever heard it. "Now darlin', before we set our minds to showing you how much we love you, grab your phone for me and write down all that information. I'll start working on it tomorrow."

Abbey went to her room to retrieve her phone.

"Duke, you don't think it could be him, do you?" I had to ask.

"Honestly, I don't know. But after what she's told us, I wouldn't put it past the bastard. I'm going to do some digging, but there is a chance it's him. It makes more sense than Grace's old trainer right now."

I felt my shoulders drop. He was right. It did make more sense. The question was, how were we going to stop the asshole and keep our woman safe?

ABBEY

Over the next week, all I could think about was that Liam and Duke loved me. I stayed in my room most of the time and painted. Liam and Duke said they wanted pictures of their horses and Jax, so I set to work on making that happen. It was going to be a surprise.

Duke and Liam still hadn't told me what the other problem was, but Duke had promised he would, so I left it alone for now. I trusted them. He had his shifts and said he was still digging into Jeff and his whereabouts. It seemed he wasn't currently in Georgia as the police there had been unable to locate him, so the search had been widened by both police forces. I decided if they didn't give me any more information by the time Duke was on his next break, then I'd push for more answers.

It was scary knowing my ex was out there somewhere, holding a grudge. On one hand, I couldn't believe after screwing other women, he'd even care to lose me. Yet on the other, Jeff hated to lose anything. And clearly that included me.

When Duke turned on my phone, I had over fifty texts from him and none of them were good.

> Jeff: What do you mean we're done? You can't walk away from me.

> Jeff: Don't think this is over, bitch. I will find you, and you'll be sorry you did this.

> Jeff: Think you're being clever? I will punish you for what you're putting me through.

> Jeff: I will have you back, one way or another. When I get my hands on you, you'll regret trying to leave me. No one leaves me.

They got worse and worse the more time passed. The voice messages were even worse. You could hear he'd been drinking in some of them, while others were clear as day and just as threatening. Duke only let me listen to a few before he took the phone away. He said he would handle everything, but I didn't want him to do this alone. I wanted to know what he was facing too, but he wouldn't tell me any details.

I shut the door behind me and smiled at the house I now thought of as mine. After being on the ranch for more than three weeks, it felt like home. Between spending time with the girls, painting, and exploring, I was happy. And after years of being unhappy, the time here felt like a gift to treasure.

I had a few minutes until I was supposed to meet Jessie at the dining hall to finish planning Blake's baby shower. As I made my way there, I waved to the ranch hands. A huge smile filled my face. I loved how close of a community it was. Part of me wished I'd come here sooner, but I know if I had, I might not have been ready to leave Jeff, and as much as it hurt, I might not have been open to being with Liam and Duke.

Jessie waved from the table in the corner where she sat waiting for me.

I jogged over. "I'm sorry to keep you waiting. Am I late?" I checked my phone to be sure I hadn't lost track of time. I'd been painting before I left, and sometimes when the muse struck, I'd be in my studio for hours.

She smiled. "Not at all. I had to finish a few things for lunch, so I was already here."

"Okay, so are we ready to finish the final details of Blake's baby shower?" I asked. I loved that Jessie asked me to help. It showed me how much they'd welcomed me with open arms.

"If the guys are okay with it, I think we should have it at your place," Jessie suggested.

"True. I'm sure I can convince them to let us use the house."

"Oh, I'm sure you can." She raised her eyebrows a few times and I couldn't help but laugh.

"Let's talk about decorations and food." I pulled out my checklist. "Since Blake doesn't know what the gender is, we need to make everything neutral. Should we go with yellow or green?"

"I think green, but we can add in other colors too. Do

we want to use a theme instead of colors? Maybe like *baby to bee* and have little bees? Or maybe *pumpkin baby*, since she's due right after Halloween."

"Oh, that's a cute idea. I like the pumpkin theme. It's still neutral, and it's holiday specific. And Blake loves pumpkin pie. We should add that to the list for food. Mini pumpkin pies would be adorable." I jotted notes, so we could keep track of what we decided. "This is going to be so much fun."

"We should pop into town tomorrow and see what we can find. Let's grab lunch with Alex and see if she has anything to add while we're there. We can also stop by Gavin's parents' house and tell them about it. I know his mom and aunt will want to be here. They're so excited."

"Once this is over, we'll need to get Tori's done before she goes into labor. I hear twins come sooner than expected." I couldn't even imagine what it felt like to have two babies.

Having babies hadn't ever crossed my mind. Although, that was likely because I knew Jeff wasn't the right guy for me. But since starting a relationship with Duke and Liam and seeing all the happy couples around the ranch, babies seemed like more of a possibility. For the first time, I could picture the three of us with a tiny little baby to love on. Did Duke and Liam want to have kids?

We discussed the remaining details of the baby shower for two more hours before it was time for Jessie to get the rest of lunch ready. I helped her prep the sandwiches. She'd made it simple, so we would have more time talking.

Duke was due home from his shift around dinnertime,

and we'd planned on having dinner in the dining hall with everyone. I still had a few hours to check on the paintings to see if they were dry enough to continue.

I made a detour through the barns to see what everyone was doing. In the second barn, I found Maverick peacefully munching on his hay. He came to the stall door to investigate if I had any treats. Which, of course, I did. He happily took the apple and completely slimed my hand as he ate it. When he was finished, I gave him a kiss on the nose before I made my way to the next barn, stopping outside to wash my hands at the hose.

Hunter and Kyle, two riders for Team Kingston, were near the wash stalls when I rounded the corner.

"Hey, guys," I called out.

"Hey, Abbey. Will you come here for a moment? Maybe you can help us with something." Kyle waved me over.

"Sure. What's up?" I wiped my hands on the sides of my pants.

"At the horse show in New York, Hunter found this amazing woman he spent the night with, and she ghosted him in the morning. He still thinks there's hope he'll see her again and thinks she could be the one for us," Kyle explained as he sprayed down his horse.

I rested a comforting hand on Hunter's arm. I hated to even have to ask this next question. "If she ghosted you, then do you think she wants to be found?"

Hunter sighed. "We had a connection that night; I'm sure of it. She told me she felt it too."

"What if you find her, and she says no?" I asked.

He ran a hand through his short, dark brown hair.

"Then I'll walk away. I'm not going to pressure her into being with us, but I want to know if there's anything I can do to help her or even give her my contact information, so she knows I want her. I can't let her slip through my fingers without trying."

I looked at Kyle to get his thoughts on this.

"I trust Hunter. He has good instincts. If he thinks she might be the one for us, I want us to follow through and see if she might want to give us a try."

"Okay, so tell me what you know about her."

"Her name is Chloe. She's sweet, determined, and a hard worker. She was one of the staff for the catering company there for the event. When I was with her, the world made sense." Hunter's eyes got a far-off look.

"That's not a lot to go off of. Didn't Tori put on the event?"

"Yes..."

"Have you asked her if she knew anyone by that name, or if she could give you the contact for the company she used for the catering? I bet they can tell you if they have an employee listed with that name. Or, if they won't give you her name because of confidentiality, they might be able to get her a message."

"I hadn't thought about that." Hunter's face lit up with the idea.

"Well, that would be where I'd start. Ask Tori. What are you going to do about the distance from New York to here? I'm guessing that's where she lives."

"If I can get a phone number, I'll start there. We have to at least try. I honestly think she is the one for us, dude."

Hunter's jaw tightened as a determined expression crossed his face.

I laughed. "I think he's got it bad, Kyle."

"Yup, and with any luck, I might be the same once we get the chance to talk to her." Kyle winked.

"Please tell me these *les jeunes* aren't bothering you." Liam wrapped his arms around me from behind, and I squealed.

"Just asking me a question," I said through a fit of laughter as he tickled my sides.

"How did your meeting with Jessie go?"

I turned in his arms to face him. "I'm all done. I just said hi to Maverick and was on my way to see if you had finished and needed anything." Reaching up, I swept his sweaty blond hair from his forehead. It was getting long enough for him to need a haircut.

"I just finished with Blake. I was going to give Zeus a bath, but it seems like these two have taken up the wash stalls." He nodded at Hunter and Kyle, who turned their hoses in our direction. I ducked for cover behind Liam, laughing as he spun around, picked me up bridal style, and rushed us into the barn.

"Liam, put me down," I squealed when we were safely in the barn.

He set me on my feet, grabbing my waist and pulling me against him. He guided me two steps back until I was pressed against the wall. "Hello, *dulcinée*." Liam lowered his head and kissed me. "Sorry, I couldn't wait any longer."

"It's okay," I said, catching my breath. My cheeks hurt

from smiling so much. Every minute was one to be cherished with him.

"Get a room, you two," someone called from the other end of the barn, and I buried my face in Liam's shirt.

"Do you need help with Zeus?" I asked.

"No, I've got it. You go home and relax. Take a nice hot bath, and I'll be home in a few hours." Liam nuzzled my neck.

"Mmm. That sounds lovely. Wish you were there to join me," I teased as I sauntered away, leaving Liam eyeing me.

I sighed. It was a shame he couldn't come with me, but I couldn't wait to soak in the tub and relax. It'd been forever since I pampered myself.

After a long soak, I decided not to go back and paint. I picked up Liam's book he left by the couch and started reading. It was a good book, but it also brought out too many scary feelings. It hit too close to home with what was happening with Jeff. Duke had mentioned they were able to find out Jeff had taken out a large sum of money, and that was it. With no credit card charges to follow or sightings of his car, he could be anywhere. However, Liam and Duke reassured me over and over they would never let Jeff get anywhere near me again.

* * *

AFTER DINNER, everyone seemed to leave the dining hall at the same time, chatting as we stopped outside the building.

"Who's ready for poker night?" Travis rubbed his hands together.

"I'm ready to take all your money, if that's what you mean." Scott gave Travis a light punch on the arm.

"You're all going down." Caleb looked around the circle, grinning.

All the girls laughed at their pre-game banter. From what Blake told me, the men played poker once a month at someone's house, and the girls got to do girl's night at another house. I'd been looking forward to relaxing with wine and a movie.

"You guys are coming too, right?" Gavin looked at Liam and Duke expectantly.

"No, we won't be able to join you," Liam said to the group.

I turned to pout at him but was caught in the burning intensity of his eyes. Hot breath fanned across my neck, sending a shiver down my spine as Duke pressed against my back.

"We have other plans for you tonight—ones that don't involve our friends," he whispered in my ear.

"Oh really. What are they?" I breathed, unable to tear my eyes away from Liam's heated gaze.

"We want to see how loud we can get you to scream our names," Duke growled.

My breath caught when he nipped my earlobe, and fire pooled between my legs. My panties were ruined, but I didn't care. I couldn't wait to see what they had planned for me.

"Rain check," Liam said.

Blake gave me a knowing look, and I knew everyone

had the correct assumption about what was about to happen. And I didn't care. I wanted it. And given how quickly we rushed home, they wanted it too.

"How do you feel about being tied up?" Liam asked the moment we stepped foot in the house.

"What?" I didn't think I heard him correctly. They wanted to tie me up?

I followed them to the bedroom, but they didn't repeat the question. Liam went to his closet and pulled out what looked like a necktie while Duke grabbed both my wrists in one hand.

"We want to know if being tied up is off the table or not," Duke growled.

"I've never done it before." I shrugged. "But I'd be willing to try it."

Liam groaned and tossed the tie to Duke. "On the bed, darlin'."

His command ignited my core. I crawled up the bed, only to be flipped by Liam. He lifted my arms over my head as Duke appeared on my other side with the tie. They worked together to secure my hands to the head-board. I gave the restraint a little tug. The bonds were firm but not tight enough that it hurt. I could still grab the slat in the headboard if my arms needed a break.

The rustling of clothes and the sounds of zippers pulled my attention from the sensation of being tied up. I licked my lips. My men stood before the bed in absolutely nothing. Their dicks were hard and pointing directly at me. Every chiseled ab was on display, and I wanted to trace every one of them with my tongue.

"Too many clothes for you, *dulcinée*. Let's fix that."

Liam undid my pants and peeled them off, along with my panties. Duke shoved my shirt and bra over my head and bunched them up them around my wrists. Rubbing my legs together, my arousal coated my thighs.

Duke dove between my legs, licking his way up my thigh. "Darlin', you taste so good."

I gasped when his hot breath fanned my pussy, and his tongue circled my clit.

"Oh my God," I moaned when he slid two fingers inside me. "Don't stop." He continued to eat me like I was his last meal while Liam ran his hands over my breasts. These two knew how to work my body.

I fought against the restraints. I wanted to grab hold of them… of something. I wrapped my hands around the slats in the headboard and used it for leverage. Arching my back, I thrust my breast up for Liam and wiggled my hips for more friction from Duke. I groaned when Duke's fingers brushed my g-spot. My body was shaking before I could stop myself.

Screaming both their names as my body spasmed, I grew light-headed, and I was excited for what they had planned. I loved knowing this was only the beginning.

Duke's fingers slid from my still pulsing pussy. Instead of pumping them back in, he lightly drew them through my folds.

He slid them between my ass cheeks, and I clenched when he settled one on my puckered hole. No one had ever touched me there before. I wasn't against it, but I was nervous about how it would feel.

"Duke," I squeaked.

He sucked my clit, sending a fresh wave of arousal

through me. Moaning, I pushed my hips toward him, feeding myself to him.

"Does that feel good?" Liam released my nipple and caught my eye. He wanted to know if I was okay with what Duke was doing.

I could barely think. I couldn't speak, so instead I gave a shy nod.

Duke's gaze met mine as he continued to lick me and lightly circle my back door. It felt so wrong, but it also felt *so right*. Nerves I didn't know I had sparked to life. Instinct took over, and I pushed my ass toward his fingers. He pressed on the ring of muscles, and my whole body zinged with a rush of pleasure.

"Fuck," I moaned.

"Do you like it?" Liam pinched my nipple before nuzzling my ear.

My whole body was alight, and I was going to come just from Duke touching me there. I nodded and bit my lip to stop from crying out when Duke tested the muscle again.

"No, *dulcinée*. We want to hear everything." Liam extracted my bottom lip from between my teeth.

"Duke, don't stop," I cried out as the need built higher and higher in my core. I needed this release. It felt different than any other I'd had.

Duke hummed, then slipped a finger into my pussy. He had two working my back entrance and two deep inside me. I didn't want him to stop. With every move he made, desire coiled within my stomach. With each pump of his hand and lick of his tongue, my body tightened. My knees pressed against Duke's ears, the sensation almost too much to handle.

My body jerked, and I let out a keening cry as I arched off the bed. My orgasm crashed through me over and over. Liam grabbed my hips and held them down for Duke to finish playing.

By the time I caught my breath, Liam was beside me, massaging my arms.

"How are you feeling, *dulcinée?*" he whispered.

"That was amazing," I breathed. I'd never have guessed how incredible that would have felt.

"Good, because it's not over." Duke grabbed my hips and flipped me, helping me to my knees.

"I want you to straddle Duke," Liam commanded. I loved when this side of him came out.

I glanced over my shoulder, but Duke gave my ass a swat before he switched places with Liam. I didn't know what either of them had in mind.

"I promise I'm not going to fuck your ass." Liam leaned over and nipped my shoulder. "At least not yet."

I moaned. It was a relief he wasn't going to do it tonight, but the swirling sensation in my stomach had me anticipating when it would come. "Thank you."

I lifted my leg, and Duke slid under me. Once he settled beneath me, he scooted us toward the headboard so my arms weren't stretched too far. Not able to hold back, I rubbed my pussy up and down his length.

"Darlin', I'm going to need you to fuck me good and hard." Duke pinched a nipple.

"Why?" I asked with a breathy moan.

"Because I'm going to play with this ass some more

while you do, and it'll be more enjoyable when you're already chasing your pleasure."

Liam went to the bedside drawer, pulling out a bottle of lube. He showed it to me, and I nodded. I loved that they wanted my permission before they tried anything new.

Duke lifted my hips and worked his cock to my opening. I slid down every inch of him with ease. He moaned, and I lifted off him only to slide down slow again.

"Fuck," he choked out.

His hands settled on my hips, lifting me and letting me drop. He sped up the pace until we were both panting. When he slowed, Liam settled behind me, and I clenched in anticipation.

"You'd better hurry, Liam. She knows what you're going to do, and she's squeezing the shit out of me right now."

Liam chuckled, running his hand down my spine. His soft touch and light kisses along my back had me relaxing and focusing on Duke once again. This time, when his hand settled low on my ass and his slippery fingers slid between my parted cheeks, I didn't flinch. Although, when he pressed against my back entrance, I clenched out of reflex.

"Look at me, darlin'." Duke tweaked my nipple. I gasped, turning my attention to the man I was riding. He swiveled his hips, hitting the sweet spot deep inside me. "It's just you and me right now. Focus on how good each slide of my cock in and out of your pussy feels."

I closed my eyes and fisted the headboard.

"Harder darlin'. Take what you need from me."

I rode Duke hard as Liam circled and pushed against the tight ring of muscle. When his finger slid past, I cried out. The feeling was intense. He worked the tip in and out, slowly sinking in deeper and deeper.

They'd wanted to hear me loud and clear, and they got it. I couldn't keep quiet even if I wanted to. My body came alive when he breached me, and I slammed down on Duke harder than before, chasing this orgasm barreling toward me.

When Liam slid a second finger in, the burn of the stretch mixed with the sparks of pleasure had me screaming out my release. I faltered as the release crashed over me, grateful when Duke took over. He gripped my hips and slammed me on his cock, holding me still as his hot cum painted my inner walls.

Liam moaned behind me, and I felt his cum splash across my back. I loved having both my men on my body. Being with them allowed me to explore my body and my sexuality in a way I never had before. That had been the best orgasm of my life, and I was completely and utterly spent. When Duke untied my restraints, I collapsed on top of him.

"Rest, *dulcinée*. You're going to need it," Liam said as the darkness took over and I fell asleep. My men had awoken something in me that was insatiable. After feeling what it was like to have Liam's fingers fucking my ass, I was no longer scared. I couldn't wait for one of them to sink deep inside me and then fuck me together.

DUKE

Since we'd found out about Abbey's ex, I dove into finding everything I could. I'd contacted the police department where he lived and had them look into him with me when we filed the restraining order. His record was squeaky clean, but he was also MIA. The police did a drop by, and it looked like he wasn't home. His job even said he put in for a last-minute vacation and hadn't reported in for three weeks. He'd taken out a large sum of money before going silent.

The timing lined up and with Abbey living with us, he was now a prime suspect for the fence and barn fire. We put a BOLO on his car and discovered he was staying in the next town over. The restraining order was easy enough to file, but we needed to pin him down to serve it.

It was time to bring Abbey into the know. We sat her down and explained everything to her, from the fence issue to the barn fire, and how we thought it might be connected to Jeff. Abbey looked like she was going to be sick.

"Darlin', are you all right?"

"It's… a lot to take in." She swallowed hard while Liam got her a glass of water. She gulped it down and it seemed to help. Taking a deep breath, Abbey turned to me.

"Why didn't you tell me before? I thought you said there were no secrets?" She punched my shoulder. She had every right to be angry with us, but it hadn't been our decision.

"Declan and Thomas didn't want anyone to know, but we thought you should, since it might be Jeff who's doing it. But you have to promise not to tell anyone else. They didn't want to worry any of the girls." I rubbed my shoulder. It hadn't hurt, but I wanted her to feel like she landed her punishment.

"*Dulcinée*, I'll be honest, I still don't want you to know. We wanted to handle your problem for you, but we also want you to be aware in case you see anything suspicious. You have to be alert until we have everything under control." Liam caught her hand. Squeezing it, he brought it to his lips and kissed her knuckles.

"I know you're only trying to protect me, but I need to protect you too. I know what he's like and what he can do. I don't want anyone to get hurt."

"We know, darlin'. And we love you for that."

"What should we do next?" She sat up straight and determination settled on her face. Abbey was preparing to do this with us, whether we wanted her to or not.

"We want to go after him while he's in our territory. If we have your permission to use your phone and message him, make him think it's you, maybe we can lure him someplace."

"The sooner we do this, the better, right? And you don't want the other girls to know?"

"Exactly. Hopefully, we can stop him before he does anything else. We don't want to stress out Blake or Tori with the news." Liam began pacing the living room. He and I agreed we didn't want to involve Abbey, but it was best if she was in the know in case something went wrong.

Abbey tapped her chin. "What about planning it for Sunday? We're doing the baby shower, and all the girls will be with me. We'll be out of the way and safe. That gives you time to trap him."

I leaned over and kissed her. "Perfect. That's a start. Now we need to lure him to us. We can message that you want to meet him. We need to plan the message, so he thinks you're sincere. Something that won't tip him off. We don't need him to try something even more dangerous than the fire." I scratched the scruff on my chin. "You know him best, Abbey. What do you suggest?"

"What were some of the last messages he sent me?" Abbey held her hand out for her phone.

My fingers gripped the plastic until the case bit into my hand. Like hell I was going to just hand it over. She knew the gist of how horrible they were, and I didn't want her to see some of the worst ones. "I'll read them to you." My voice sounded gruff, even to my ears.

Her eyes softened. "He can't hurt me anymore. Not now. Not after being with the two of you."

I sighed. "Abbey, some of these messages are beyond hurtful. I can't let you see them."

She set her hand on my knee. "Okay. I get it."

Turning the phone on, I pulled up the last few messages.

> Jeff: Abbey, I know this isn't you. You're letting Blake and Grace into your head, and you don't want that. You know you belong with me.

> Jeff: Abbey, come home and I'll forgive you for everything.

> Jeff: I need to see you again. I miss you so much. You left me without so much as a goodbye. You have to come back to me.

At least the last three weren't so bad. I turned the phone so Abbey could read the messages, and she rolled her eyes. I bit back my laughter.

"We need to play nice, right?" She glanced at me and then back to the screen.

I tilted my hand from side to side. "Basically." I didn't want to play nice with the fucker, but we had to remain calm for this to work.

Liam pointed at the phone. "How about agreeing to meet with him? Nothing more, nothing less."

"I think we need a little more than that. If we say okay, I'll come see you, it'll be suspicious." My mind was trying to find the best angle. All my training in the military and police academy told me we needed more—more help, more time, more resources, more everything.

"How about we keep it simple? I tell him I regret leaving and I'm okay with meeting him so we can talk it out." Abbey pursed her lips.

I nodded. I hated hearing her say that, even though it was a lie. This situation with Jeff couldn't be over soon enough.

"What about this?" Abbey grabbed the phone and typed a reply. She handed it back when she was done and waited for me to read it. I made a small tweak, then showed her the revision. When she nodded, I then showed Liam. He pursed his lips but caved.

"Let's send it. We don't want to wait. I know how quickly his moods can change." Abbey worried her bottom lip.

She was right. I'd read through all the other messages. Jeff was sweet one second and a total psychopath the next.

> Abbey: Hi, Jeff. I've been thinking you might be right. I'd like to talk with you about us.

I hit send, and we waited patiently for his reply.

> Jeff: I'm happy you're finally seeing reason.

> Abbey: Where do you want to meet? I talked to my mom, and I'm guessing you might be nearby based on what she said.

I showed the messages to them. When they both nodded, I hit send.

> Jeff: There's a hotel by the highway about thirty minutes north. Room four-thirty-two. Come alone.

"What time is the baby shower?" I asked Abbey.

"Eleven-thirty."

"Let's tell him noon. That way, we can be far away when this goes down, and you'll all be at the shower." My fingers hovered over the keyboard.

"That'll work," Liam said.

> Abbey: I can come on Sunday around noon. Send me the address.

> Jeff: Fine, but don't be late. You know how much I hate that.

> Abbey: I'll be right on time. See you Sunday.

Jeff replied with the address for the hotel, and I made note of it in my phone.

We all took a deep breath. Phase one was in motion. He agreed to meet us. Now we had to work on backup in case anything went sideways. Even though I was a sheriff, there were still rules that needed to be followed. We had the restraining order, but I couldn't deliver it alone. I was too involved.

Pulling out my phone, I shot Thomas a message.

> Duke: We think the intruder is after Abbey. An ex of hers who followed her here.

> Thomas: How do you want to handle it?

> Duke: We want to set a trap for him, but we're going to need some help.

> Thomas: What kind of help?

> Duke: Police from town. We want to serve him the restraining order, but when we do, I'll also need to question him about the ranch.

> Thomas: Do what needs to be done, but make sure we don't draw too much attention to the ranch. Tell me the place and time. I'll be nearby to make sure he doesn't try to cry foul.

> Duke: Got it, boss. Thanks.

Now that I had Thomas' approval, I wanted to move forward. I'd call the station in the morning and work out the details. Tonight, Liam and I would spread the word to the men around the ranch about what was going on, and hopefully, with more eyes on watch, nothing else would occur. That was our biggest fear—that Jeff would figure out we were playing him and he'd retaliate.

I was itching to round him up immediately, but I knew we had to wait. Even with Abbey safely with us in the house, I still wasn't settled. I wouldn't be until the guy was behind bars for hurting my woman.

After a restless night, I called the station and set up a meeting for the afternoon to discuss a plan. Liam and I wanted to get with the other guys before I left to fill them in on everything.

"Are you going to Blake's?" Abbey peeked into my office.

"Yes. We're going to fill Gavin and Travis in on what's going on. I have the meeting this afternoon in town. I'll have more information to give everyone else."

"Can I come with you? I want to see Blake and pick her brain about something."

"Sure. I'm leaving in a minute. Are you ready?" I strode over and planted a kiss on her forehead.

"Ready when you are." She beamed. My heart filled with warmth. Seeing her smiling and not so hesitant was everything. She was my world. Why I wanted to fight it those first few days was beyond me. I couldn't imagine my life without her now.

ABBEY

$\mathcal{I}$ stared at the pregnancy tests in my hand. The little pink plus signs had my stomach churning. When I met with Blake last week, I realized when we were pouring over our planners and talking about schedules that I'd missed my period. I was three days late.

I tried to tell myself it was no biggie. Except I'd never been late in my life. The guys and I still hadn't had the conversation about whether or not we all wanted to have kids.

Randomly going into town might bring questions I wasn't ready to answer. I also didn't want to stress Liam or Duke out before they met with Jeff. I'd told Blake I needed to borrow a sweater of hers yesterday when me and the guys had stopped by. When she went to grab it, I excused myself to use the restroom.

Weeks ago, Blake had jokingly asked what to do with all the leftover pregnancy tests she hadn't used. The rest of the girls told her to keep them for next time and laughed. I was forever grateful I knew they even existed. I dug through Blake's cabinet until I found a box.

The first stupid test didn't have a solid plus sign, so I took another one. When the second one gave a firm positive, I knew it was real.

I was pregnant.

It was either Duke or Liam's. Jeff and I hadn't slept together for months.

With all the stress of everything going on, I didn't want to tell anyone, so I hid the tests in my bag and went home.

The pounding on the front door and Jax's barking had me shoving the tests back in my bag and shaking off the feeling that something bad was going to happen. I didn't know if the guys wanted kids, if they wanted to start this soon, or if they wanted a family period. There was a lot to talk about, but not now. Not when they were on their way to arrest Jeff and Blake's baby shower was about to begin.

Today was about Blake. Not me.

This party would be a good distraction. Jessie had made herself at home in the kitchen, putting together food, and Grace was serving up drinks. I opened the door, revealing Blake and the rest of the girls.

"Oh my gosh, you guys. This is amazing," Blake squealed when she stepped inside. Jessie and I had gone with the pumpkin theme like we discussed and had little pumpkins scattered everywhere. The banner across the wall read A LITTLE PUMPKIN IS ON THE WAY.

We ate, drank, and opened presents. Blake's mother-in-law, Gavin's mom, and aunt-in-law came for the shower, and Blake looked so happy to have them here. Seeing other family members accept the different lifestyle gave me hope my mom would be as understanding.

When we settled down and had cake, I couldn't hold it in any longer. I'd tried to stop myself, but the worry was too strong to ignore the constant pregnancy thoughts circling my brain. I was going to burst if someone didn't know soon. "When you told the guys you were pregnant, were you afraid they'd be upset?" I caught Blake's gaze.

"Well, no. We'd been trying for a few months when it happened." Blake's forehead creased. "Why?"

I set my hand on my abdomen. "Because I'm scared to tell Duke and Liam."

I was tackled by Grace first. The scent of the lotion she always wore filled my nose. She crushed me with her hug only to relinquish me to another person. Everyone spouted their congratulations, but I felt like something was missing.

"I'm so sorry for turning the attention to me," I told Blake. "Today is your day. I was just so sick to my stomach, I couldn't hold it in anymore." I raised tear-filled eyes to my friend.

"Oh, Abbey, please don't say that. You have nothing to be sorry about." She squeezed me as tight as she could with her baby belly between us.

"Why would you be worried?" Jessie settled next to me on the couch.

"Because I don't know how they'll react. I mean, we haven't talked about our future, and I'm scared they'll be angry. It wasn't planned." I blinked rapidly at the ceiling to try to stop the tears.

"Honey, they will be thrilled. Liam and Duke are both family men. Even though Duke might not show it, I know him." Jessie rubbed my back.

"Sweetheart, I've watched Duke grow up. I promise you he is going to be over the moon," Gavin's mother chimed in. The pit in my stomach lessened, knowing the two people who knew Duke the longest said everything would be okay.

"And I've known Liam for forever," Blake added. "He's always wanted a big family. He's going to be so excited when you tell him."

I had a feeling Liam was going to be the easy one, but it still made me nervous to tell them.

"How long have you known?" Tori asked.

"Since yesterday. I took the tests when I was at Blake's." I turned to her. "By the way, I'm sorry. I stole a few tests from you."

Blake laughed. "I wish you'd told me. I'd have been there to hold your hand while you waited for the tests to tell you yes or no."

"I know. I was afraid to say the words out loud."

"I'm so happy for you. This is all Grace and I've ever wanted for you. You have two men who adore you, and now you're going to start a family. I'm so proud of you for grabbing hold of the life you deserve." Blake wiped her eyes.

"Okay, we have way too many hormonal women in this room right now." Alex laughed, not bothering to hide her tears.

A pounding on the door startled us all. "Were we expecting someone? Maybe one of the other guys on the ranch decided to crash our party." Jessie laughed as she opened the door. Before she got to it, it flung open and bounced off the wall. In barged a man I knew all too well. He shoved Jessie aside and headed straight into the living room. Panic skittered down my spine as I faced the man I never wanted to see again.

Jeff.

I leapt to my feet. My mind raced with all the unanswered questions, along with the fear that he might hurt someone. He was supposed to be at the hotel.

"What are you doing here?" My voice shook. This was not good. If Jeff was here, what happened to Duke and Liam?

"Oh, Abbey. You know better than to ask stupid questions." Jeff pulled a gun from behind his back, keeping it against his leg.

The girls screamed and huddled together.

"*Quiet!*" Jeff roared.

"Why are you here?" I asked again.

"You really think your little trick was going to work on me? You think I didn't suspect you were trying to set me up?" He waved the gun in the air. "Those guys are on a wild goose chase."

I breathed a small sigh. That meant he hadn't hurt either Duke or Liam. They were still safe.

"Let everyone go. This is between you and me."

"I don't think so. You think I want them all running to their men?" Jeff spat. "I know what goes on around here. I've been watching you for weeks. The little whores can stay where they are."

"Jeff, you know some of them," I pleaded, hoping to

appeal to some hidden sense of decency he might have possessed. "Blake is pregnant. Tori is too. Please let them out of here. This is not good for the babies."

"No." The vein on his forehead pulsed. He was getting ready to rage. My worst fear was he'd hurt one of them. I needed him to focus on me. Taking a few deep breaths, I tried to calm the panic threatening to take over. I had to think of something, anything, to get the girls out of here.

But I could only come up with one thing, and it tore my heart apart just thinking it.

I was going to have to give myself to him. It was the only way to get his focus solely on me and get him off the ranch as quickly as possible. And that meant leaving Liam and Duke.

A wave of nausea fought its way up my throat. I swallowed hard, forcing it down.

"Let them go, Jeff, and I'll leave with you."

"Abbey, no!" Blake shouted behind me.

His laugh was unhinged. "You were coming with me either way. You really thought you had a say in that? You *belong* to me, not these assholes. They stole you from me, and I'm here to bring you home."

He huffed out a breath. I could tell he was still angry, but he was collecting himself. He usually did when I obeyed him. Hopefully, by acquiescing immediately, he'd lessen the blow when he punished me.

"Blake, Grace." He looked at the other girls behind me. "Don't say I never did anything nice. Go before I change my mind."

I didn't turn around. I could hear the scurrying of their feet as everyone rushed for the front door. Out of the corner of my eye, I could see Blake and Tori being helped out first, followed by the remaining women. Grace lingered behind. I knew she didn't want to leave me with him.

"Go, Grace. I'll be fine." I gave her a forced smile. I would be fine. I had to be. This little baby growing inside me needed me to be strong.

She hesitated a moment longer but finally left. I let out a breath of relief. Everyone was safe.

Once the girls were gone, Jeff ran to the front door and locked it. "I don't need anyone barging in here."

His shoulders relaxed a little. He was calmer than I'd expected. He walked past me, then paused.

"Oh, and Abbey…?"

"Yes." I looked at him, catching the devilish smile stretched across his face.

His hand came out of nowhere. The sting on my cheek took me by surprise. In the past, I'd been able to anticipate when he'd strike me and at least try to prepare myself.

He grabbed my jaw, forcing me to look at him. "That was for running away. You know better than that." He sighed and shook his head, giving me a disappointed look. "But don't think you're getting off that easy. We don't have time here. You'll get your punishment when we get home."

Jeff pushed me away from him. I stumbled and fell to the ground, landing on my wrist, crying out when a sharp pain shot through my hand. Cradling my arm, I watched as Jeff went down the hall and into the guest bedroom, which was now my studio.

Carefully, I followed him. What was he doing? Weren't we supposed to be leaving? I wanted to get him as far away as possible to keep everyone else safe. The longer we were here, the greater the risk to the other girls.

The closer I got to my studio, the louder the thuds sounded behind the wall. Jeff's grunt of anger ripped through me, making me pause in fear. I should see what he was doing, but what if he tried to hurt me again?

I turned the corner to walk into the guest room and froze.

"What are you doing? Jeff, stop!" I screamed, realizing too late that challenging him was not the best move.

Jeff had ripped apart the canvases, thrown paints around the room, and started lighting the drapes and bed sheets on fire.

"I'm erasing you from this place," he said with no inflection in his tone. No anger or frustration. It was then I realized how truly psychotic he was. How had I taken this long to see there was something wrong with him?

"But this is *their* house. They'll forget all about me. You don't need to destroy their home. Please, let's go." I grabbed his arm with my good hand and tried to pull him. The smoke coming from the burning textiles was already making me cough. Inhaling the acrid smell wasn't good for me or the baby. I needed to get Jeff out of here.

"Why? What do they mean to you?" He pulled me against him and looked me in the eyes. His face scrunched with rage and his body trembled. "You *love* them?"

"I don't, I promise," I pleaded.

This time I saw his hand, but I wasn't able to dodge it.

When his fist hit my jaw, I tasted blood. Sweat rolled down my back as the curtains and blankets were engulfed with flames. The paint was likely accelerating the spread of the fire.

"Fine, if you love them, then stay here. Consider this your punishment for loving them." Jeff shoved me farther into the room and shut the door. "See if their love can save you from this," he shouted.

I tried the handle, but Jeff must have wedged something beneath the knob.

I looked around for another way out, but the window was surrounded by burning curtains. The painted canvases caught fire easily, and I wanted to cry as the edges curled up and disappeared underneath the orange and red flames. I coughed and crouched to the floor. I had nothing to break the window with. I was truly trapped. Turning to the door, I banged my good hand on it and yelled for help.

The entire bed had caught fire, and it was snaking up the wall. Smoke clouded the room, and I searched the floor for a rag to put over my mouth. I almost cried with relief when my fingers touched the soft cotton of my t-shirt. I'd been hot the other day and yanked the shirt off, not bothering to see where it landed.

Hope was beginning to fizzle out. My chest tightened with the lack of clean air, and despair consumed my mind. I lay flat on the floor and reminded myself there was still time for me to be saved.

I regretted wasting so much mental energy worrying about telling them I was pregnant. I'd been so afraid they'd reject me. I'd never fully given them my trust, even though they were out there fighting my battles for me. At least I'd gotten to tell them I loved them before they left.

The fire spread, inching toward the door. I backed away as much as possible, but I was surrounded. It was getting harder and harder to breathe, even as I covered my face with my shirt. I fought against the darkness creeping in.

"Abbey!" a muffled voice called out.

"Abbey, where are you?" another person yelled. I wanted to respond, but my vocal cords seized.

The room was hazy, and I wasn't sure if I imagined it when I saw the door open. The shadowy figure in the doorway rushed in, scooped me up, and charged past men coming into the house with a hose and what looked like fire extinguishers.

I buried my nose in my rescuer's neck. I wasn't sure who'd gotten me to safety. The light was so bright outside, I had to shield my face with my hand. The identity of my savior would remain a mystery for a few more seconds. My focus was on trying to breathe. Now that we were outside, a blast of fresh air hit me, and I gasped, then a wracking cough shook my body.

My rescuer, who I now recognized as Gavin, set me on the tailgate of a truck. Matt stood next to him, placing an oxygen mask on my face. My brain was still foggy, I assumed it was from the smoke.

"Abbey, breathe slowly. Look at me." Gavin's commanding tone soothed me only a little. I took slow, deep breaths, barely registering anything else around me. I needed to find my voice so I could ask about Liam and Duke and if my baby was going to be okay.

When the fog cleared, I noticed the girls in the background, forced to stay far away. It was a relief to see that everyone had gotten away safely. The house was still on fire, but the water truck they used to water the nearby pastures during droughts was being used to help fight the flames. I had to wonder how long it would take for the fire crew to get here to finish the job.

I stared at the house as it continued to burn. Tears streamed down my face as I saw the only place I'd ever felt safe being destroyed. Duke and Liam's home was gone. My new beginning was over. I couldn't take my eyes off it, even as the lights and sirens came up behind me.

Eventually, an EMT arrived and assessed me. I was still in a daze when I was moved to the back of the ambulance. Lights shined in my eyes, my wrist was wrapped, cuts were being cleaned, but all I could think about was I was out of there... but Jeff was still free. Once he found out I escaped, he would be back. I trembled at the fear that ripped through me and tightened my stomach. A blanket was wrapped around me, but the shivering didn't stop.

"What can you tell us, Colt?" Gavin asked the EMT.

"Minor smoke inhalation. You guys got her out before anything serious happened. A few cuts, bruises, minor burns, and a sprained wrist, but otherwise, nothing major. She doesn't need to go to the ER, but she will need to follow up tomorrow with Doc." Colt gave his report in a matter-of-fact tone.

"She's pregnant. Very early. Do you think this will have any effect on the baby?" Blake's voice filtered through my thoughts. I turned to her, and a fresh wave of tears fell.

I stuttered, "I-is the baby going to be okay?"

Blake, with the assistance of Gavin, climbed onto the back of the ambulance and wrapped her arms around me. We silently rocked back and forth as Colt responded. "I can't say for certain. She needs to follow up with Doc. Same goes for you and Tori. And the rest of the girls," Colt ordered.

"Don't worry. We'll have them in his office first thing in the morning. You have my word." Gavin shook Colt's hand and let the EMT depart.

"Abbey?" My heart nearly stopped when I heard Liam's voice. I extracted myself from Blake's arms in time to see Duke and Liam running toward me.

DUKE

$\mathcal{W}$e really thought we'd been one step ahead of Jeff, but the asshole played us. He checked into the hotel but never stayed. So, of course the credit card pinged on the BOLO we'd put out for him when we double checked the address. Using my badge, I had the room attendant let us in. The room looked like it was never even slept in.

My gut churned. I wanted to get back home to Abbey. Something wasn't right. We needed to ensure Abbey was safe. There were too many miles between us and her for my liking.

As we neared the ranch, the other station cars sped by with their lights flashing. The blood in my veins froze. I turned my radio up to hear the chatter.

"Fire at King's Ranch is under control. Only minor injuries reported," the dispatcher relayed.

I looked at Liam. "Did she just say fire at King's Ranch?"

"Yes, step on it." Liam's face showed the horror and

fear I knew coursed through me. I slammed my foot on the accelerator and sped as fast as I could toward the ranch.

We turned into the entrance, the car bumping along the road. Once we were close enough, the smoke plume grew larger and larger. My heart pounded in my chest. What had happened? Where was the fire? Was Abbey okay?

We headed straight for the flashing lights of the fire trucks and ambulance. My heart nearly stopped when we could make out that it was our house that had been on fire.

I veered off the dirt road and into the grass near the barn. Quickly putting the car in park, I jumped out, seconds behind Liam as we sprinted to our house.

"Abbey," I shouted. Searching the faces out front, I didn't see her. I caught sight of Scott, who pointed toward the ambulance. No. Please no. If we lost her now, I'd never recover.

Turning, we headed toward the truck. Abbey was sitting on the edge of the bumper just inside the open doors. I let out a breath. She was safe, she was whole, she was alive.

"Abbey," Liam shouted. Abbey turned in our direction. When she saw us, her face lit up before crumpling. Soot streaked across her face and her clothes. I needed to have her in my arms or I'd lose it. She threw off the blanket she was wrapped in and ran to us. When she reached Liam, she leaped into his arms, wrapping her legs around him. Their lips locked in a desperate kiss—one we all needed.

I stood back for a second and assessed her. Her wrist

was wrapped, and she had a few other bandages, but she was safe.

I stepped up beside them, and Abbey broke the kiss, turning to me. The sight of her face had me pulling back. I could see the bruise forming on her cheekbone and the split lip. My blood boiled. Now I knew why Jeff didn't meet us. I was going to kill him for laying a hand on our girl.

Liam set Abbey down, and we both ran our fingers over her body to make sure she was all right. Liam gingerly took her wrapped wrist and kissed her hand.

"I'm okay, guys. Now that you're both here, everything is going to be okay." I could see the uncertainty in her eyes though. I needed to know what happened. Was she afraid we couldn't protect her?

The sound of a throat clearing broke the moment. We'd have to wait until we were alone to find out what she was thinking. We turned to see Colt, the local EMT, waiting to give us an update.

"Tell us she's okay," Liam begged.

"Minor smoke inhalation. She's really lucky the guys got her out before anything serious happened. A few bruises, scrapes, and a couple of minor burns. She has a sprained wrist that should heal soon, but otherwise nothing major. She doesn't need to go to the ER, but she needs to be monitored for shock and for smoke inhalation. Her lungs will be sore for the next few days," Colt said. "Do not leave her alone. She needs to follow up with Doc in the morning. Gavin assured me that all the girls would report in."

There was no way I was letting Abbey out of my sight.

They'd have to pry me away from her. And we'd make sure she made it to that appointment.

The fire chief came over and gave us an update as well. The fire was out, but they weren't able to save the house. Too much structural damage. I appreciated his sympathy, but it didn't matter. The house could be rebuilt; Abbey was irreplaceable.

After the report from the fire crew and EMT, we still hadn't heard anything about what had actually occurred. With Abbey safely tucked under my arm, I steered us toward the group of men nearby. Gavin, Ty, and Travis were giving their statements to the officers who responded to the call. They all looked like they'd just went through hell.

"What the fuck happened?" I asked the moment Gavin was able to break free and approach us.

"According to the girls, Jeff barged in on the baby shower and held Abbey hostage. Everyone ran to Ty's place and told him Jeff was in the house." I squeezed Abbey closer to my side as Gavin told the story. "Ty called the police, and Scott ran to round up anyone he could find. We surrounded the house just in time for Jeff to sneak out the back door. Travis and Kyle were the closest and tackled him to the ground. They got him tied up before he could get far."

"Don't worry. He's already in the back of my patrol car, locked up tight," Charlie, one of the other officers, said. I'd been so worried about Abbey I hadn't even noticed they'd apprehended Jeff.

I tightened my grip on Abbey. It took everything in me to stop myself from yanking him from the car and beating the shit out of him, but Abbey clung to me, and she was my lifeline to remaining calm. I knew it wasn't what she would want. Especially if it got me in trouble with the law. I could almost hear her voice in my head telling me it wasn't worth it. Jeff wasn't worth it.

"When we saw smoke from the guest bedroom window, we ran in to find Abbey," Gavin continued. "She was locked in there, and I brought her outside while some of the other men worked on putting out the fire."

My chest tightened at the thought of almost losing her tonight.

"I'm so sorry we couldn't save the house." Gavin put his hand on Liam's shoulder. I knew he didn't care about the house. His eyes were glued to Abbey.

Abbey collapsed in my arms. Liam and some of the other men rushed to catch her as well, but I had her. I wasn't letting her go.

"Darlin', are you okay? Do you need the doctor?" My voice was laced with panic as I cradled her against me.

Abbey shook her head.

"What's wrong then?" Liam's voice rivaled mine.

"It's over. It's finally over." She smiled.

She was right. They caught Jeff. No matter how much I wanted to do it myself, it was done. Jeff was going to jail, with no chance of getting out. Multiple accounts of domestic abuse and now attempted murder, not to mention arson. No doubt once an investigation was opened, he'd be pinned for the other things as well.

Abbey planted a searing kiss on my lips. All I could do was hold her against me. She was safe in my arms, and I was never going to let her go. Every day, she'd know just how special she was. I loved her more than words could express.

"I hate we weren't here to keep you safe," I whispered against her lips.

Abbey pulled back, her eyebrows knitting together.

"Duke, I love you. You can't be by my side all the time."

I made sure she was steady on her feet before grasping her arms and staring into her eyes.

"I can't bear the thought of what might have happened if everyone else hadn't been here." My voice cracked.

Abbey cupped my cheek in her hands. "We have an incredible group of friends who are here for us, no matter what. And you were keeping me safe by going to the hotel. We could never have guessed Jeff would come here."

I nodded. She was right. I'd been thinking I had to do everything on my own. The only reason I allowed my fellow police officers to be part of the hotel setup was because I needed to make sure everything was on the up and up so we could arrest him. If I'd been more open to having help, I'd have made sure the guys were on the lookout for Jeff too.

Abbey pulled Liam into our embrace. "I love both of you. There was no way you would've known this was going to happen. None of this is your fault. It's all mine for bringing it to all of you."

Liam tightened his arms around us. "*Dulcinée*, this is not your fault. Like you said, no one could have guessed this would happen. The most important thing is we came out the other side together."

"I love you." I captured Abbey's lips in a soft kiss

before passing her to Liam to steal one as well. "Will you stay with us forever?" I hadn't planned on saying it now, or in this situation, but I knew the timing was right. We needed to know for sure that Abbey was staying with us. I needed to hear her say it and to make sure she realized we wanted her in our lives.

Abbey gazed at me. "What?"

"We can't let you go. We love you. You are the one for us, and we don't want to lose you. Please stay with us. Live with us. Be our wife," Liam responded.

"We want you with us for forever. Will you marry us?" I said.

Abbey looked between Liam and me. "Yes, yes, yes." Her lips trembled as she whispered the words, and tears streamed down her face.

I pulled her in and sealed it with another kiss, trying to be careful of her injuries. My heart pounded in my chest. Nothing could beat this feeling. The woman we loved had agreed to marry us.

Liam took Abbey away for his own kiss.

"We can build a new house. Build you a studio. Whatever you want, it's yours." I wanted to start new. I had never truly envisioned building a family in the house Liam and I had originally built. Now we could start over and have a proper home.

"I was kind of thinking maybe we could also add another room." Abbey gave a shy smile. "For a nursery."

I grinned. I loved that idea, and the first chance we got, I'd love to make sure we got Abbey pregnant.

"Anything you want, *dulcinée*." A huge grin stretched across Liam's face.

"And maybe we finish it sooner rather than later." She bit her lip, her worried gaze bounced back and forth between us.

It took me a few seconds to register what she'd said. "Really?"

Abbey let her hands drop to rest against her stomach.

"You're pregnant?" My face stretched, and my smile likely rivaled Liam's.

Abbey grinned.

I picked Abbey up and spun her around. Abbey loved us, she had agreed to marry us, and she was going to have our baby. Life couldn't get any better than this. Joy tingled along every one of my nerve endings.

"Hell yes!" Liam hollered, drawing the attention of our friends.

Abbey was giggling by the time I put her down.

"How long have you known?" Liam cupped her face.

"A day. I missed my period, but I wasn't sure how to tell you." She worried her lip between her teeth.

I tilted her chin up. "Never be afraid to tell us something. No matter what it is, we'll be there for each other and figure it out. But this, darlin'? This is the best news you could ever have given us."

"I won't. From now on, we're a team. I love you both so much." She ran one hand along my cheek and one on Liam's.

"This is the greatest gift, *dulcinée*. And tomorrow we're going to make sure you are at the doctor's office first thing in the morning."

Abbey laughed. "Let Blake and Tori go first. They take priority."

"No one is more important than you are." I tapped Abbey on the nose.

"I love you guys." She sighed. "Thank you for rescuing me."

"Thank you for saving us right back." She had no idea how true that statement was. I had a new lease on life, and it was all because of her. And Liam's heart that had wanted to find our love so badly, was finally content.

We watched the fire trucks and ambulances drive away. Those we knew waved goodbye, their faces grim with the sight of our home in tatters behind us. They didn't realize we looked at this as a new beginning, not an ending. I snuggled Abbey from behind, keeping my arms tight around her, my palms covering her belly. It was amazing to think our baby was growing right there.

Thomas clapped a hand to my back. "Stay at our place until this gets sorted out."

I looked at Liam to see if he was on board.

"We'd appreciate that," Liam answered.

"We're family," Declan reminded us. "We're here for whatever you need."

"Thank you both," Abbey responded, and I could picture a smile on her beautiful face.

They both wished us congratulations as they dispersed and went to their home, giving us a few minutes of alone time.

Liam grabbed Abbey's hand and kissed her knuckles. "Come on, let's relax. I still need to check every inch of our future wife's body to make sure she's not hurt anywhere else." He waggled his eyebrows, and Abbey and I both laughed.

It felt good to laugh.

"Maybe we can see how loud we can make her scream before the Kingstons kick us out," I said, leading the way to the big house.

The three of us walked together as we made our new path for our future.

* * *

WANT to see a glimpse of the future that awaits this hot trio? Get my Bonus Epilogue for *Rescuing Abbey,* exclusively for my newsletter subscribers.

Catch up with this trio and dive into even more sexy stories in Book Six in the King's Ranch series coming Summer 2024.

ACKNOWLEDGMENTS

This book would not have been possible without the support of my favorite writing group. Thank you to- Aidy Award, Stephanie Fanning Harrell, JL Madore, Daphine Gooch, Dylan Crush, and Kaci Rose. Thank you for writing with me every day and helping me write through my pregnancy.

I also want to thank all my amazing readers. Without you, I would not be where I am today. It is an honor to write for you and it is a dream that you love my stories as much as you do. I promise you, there are a few more stories left to tell.

ABOUT THE AUTHOR

Danielle was raised in Texas and grew up working with horses. Her love for horses and reading romance novels inspired a dream and sparked an idea for a book. Which then turned into a series of sexy cowboys and the loves of their lives getting happy ever afters.

Connect with Danielle on her website: https://www. authordaniellehart.com or on social media. She loves to hang out with readers in her exclusive reader group on Facebook

Join her newsletter for updates on when all her books come out, sneak peeks of her current work in progress and you'll get a free novella set at King's Ranch.

Made in the USA
Las Vegas, NV
17 August 2024